UROBOROS

THE CIRCLE OF TIME

First edition published by Chickpea Press Ltd, 2019
www.chickpeapress.co.uk

© Tania Henzell-Thomas, 2018

ISBN: 978-0-9571388-5-8

A CIP catalogue record for this book is available at the British Library.

The cover design is based on two paintings by Cara Helminski Chadwick: 'Freyja' and 'Uroboros'. The chapter headings also feature a design based on 'Uroboros'.
www.caragracefineart.com

Design consultant: Clare Thorpe.

Design by Daniel Thomas Dyer.

UROBOROS

THE CIRCLE OF TIME

Tania Henzell-Thomas

Chickpea Press

*With deepest gratitude
to my husband and soulmate, Jeremy,
for all the loving help and support
he has given me over the years.*

Chapter I

His toes sank into the soft, warm sand and the sea lapped gently around his ankles, as he stood looking out across the water. Somehow, he didn't know how, he knew that this vast ocean covered more than half the great sphere on which he lived. The water was as clear as crystal, and shoals of small fish swam fearlessly around him, their bodies shimmering with incandescent colours, as he stood, motionless, thinking, longing, for what he did not know. Seaweed trailed through the water like strands of long, green hair tugged by the gentle swirls and eddies of the incoming tide, which sighed and gasped like the breath of a huge, enigmatic creature.

It was a soft, soothing sound, which lulled his troubled mind. He could not remember ever having feelings like this before. He had lived here, at ease and untroubled for—he could not remember a beginning, nor a time when things had been different. But now there were dreams, visions of a desolate place filled with strange, upright creatures who walked on two legs as he did, and yet there was something very different about them. He could not see clearly as a dark mist swirled around their faces, but he knew that they were afraid, and that they were searching for something, but neither he nor they knew what it was.

He had asked and asked what this could mean, but this time there had been no answer. Usually, if he was unsure of anything, he asked a question silently in his mind and the knowledge would come. There was not an animal, bird, or fish that he did not know. He knew their calls and could answer them. He knew where each creature lived and what it ate, when it was looking for a mate, and when its young would be born. He knew where each plant grew, when it would flower, and when it would bear fruit. He knew when the rain would fall, and when the winds would blow. But he did not know where these strange visions came from.

The sun rose higher in the clear blue sky and sent rays of gold and silver light shimmering across the water. A gentle breeze blew and ruffled his hair. He grinned. It was the west wind, always gentle and warm. He turned and waded towards the beach, savouring the feeling of the warm water moving against his shins.

He was a tall man, his skin bronzed by the sun and a life lived wholly in the open air. The trees and the natural caves beneath the cliffs were his home. He had no need of any other kind of shelter. His hair grew in long, gentle curls which cascaded down his back. He looked neither young nor old, yet his eyes reflected the kind wisdom and depth which could only have come with the passing years. He walked with youthful energy and enthusiasm as he made his way inland to the top of a nearby hill.

Sometimes he would sit on the top of this particular hill and talk to the winds. The west wind was soft and warm and spoke to him with a gentle voice filled with the scent of jasmine. The north wind was sharp and cold, full of icy exuberance which lifted and energised him. The south wind was hot and dry, its breath carrying with it an air of melancholic longing which tugged at his heart. But his favourite, the east wind, was warm and full of surprises, sometimes drenching him with a sudden downpour of soft rain. He smiled as he remembered the last time he had laughed and run with the four winds blowing and chasing around him, calling each one in turn.

For a while he forgot his troubling dreams as he stood on the hill top looking out over the surrounding countryside, the four winds chasing and buffeting around him. In one direction a vast forest stretched as far as the eye could see. Great, moisture-filled clouds drifted above the tree tops, giving the whole scene a hazy, dreamlike appearance. And if he turned around and faced east, there was the glistening water of the ocean, smooth and warm as burnished copper beneath the rays of the setting sun. Occasionally, he saw the arched back of a large fish as it breached the surface then plunged back into the depths. Flocks of sea birds circled and soared over the rocks around the shore, calling to one another as they hung on the warm air, wings still and outstretched, supported by the wind.

He knew that soon they would start to lay their eggs on the cliff tops, and then he would see the young ones hatch. He loved to climb the cliffs and visit their nests, where he could watch them turn from tiny, helpless little creatures into large, handsome adult birds.

He watched as flocks of small birds on their way to roost for the night swirled and swooped around the tree tops, forming strange shapes as they flew. Sometimes they flew in his direction, seeming to hover just in front of him, where this living cloud of birds momentarily took the shape of a man, a flower, a fish, then a bird. When he thought of a shape, there it was before him, hanging, suspended in the air, hundreds of tiny winged creatures moving as one. Then they turned and flew off in the direction of a large tree, where they alighted, twittering and calling to each other sleepily.

Now the light was fading, and it was time for him too to find a place to spend the night. Usually he would curl up beneath a tree, lying on the soft moss which grew there. So he made his way down the hill towards the forest, where he found a comfortable spot, and just as the last rays of the sun dipped behind the hill, causing it to form a dark shape against the red sky, he closed his eyes and surrendered himself to sleep, lulled by the gentle sounds of the night creatures around him.

Strange, harsh, strident sounds. What were they? No animal or bird that he knew of made such sounds. They ripped and tore through his dreams, roaring and raging, until he woke, staring wildly around him. But there was nothing there, only the peace of the forest, filled with the night sounds of birds and small creatures rustling through the undergrowth. Images from his dream filled his head; vague, dark images of the frightened, two-legged creatures and some other, peculiar animals. At least he took them to be animals, although they were very large, and their hairless skins shone with an unnaturally cold smoothness that made him shiver. It was these creatures that made the sounds that he had heard in his dream. What were they? Some were tearing along a smooth, narrow grey plain, lines of them one behind the other. Still more of them formed another, similar line coming from the opposite direction but still keeping to this narrow flat plain, even though open ground stretched out on either side of them, where they could easily have run free. Others, which must be huge birds he thought, flew through the air making a terrible roaring sound as they went. The sound was so loud that it made the air vibrate, rending it apart like a huge crash of thunder, and he saw other, more familiar birds flying in panic away from the huge beasts.

Gradually, the peace of his surroundings calmed him, and he fell asleep again. But the dream returned, only this time he saw huge structures with more of the two-legged animals walking between them. The structures looked a little like hills, but they did not undulate gently and were not covered with soft, green grass and trees like the hills he knew. They were barren and cold. No soft earth for small creatures to burrow into. No warm rocks for the lizards and insects to bask on. Perhaps they were caves, he thought, as some of them appeared to have openings in them, and the two-legs were going in and out. There were some caves up on the cliffs. He had seen them when he visited the sea birds' nests in the spring. But those caves had large openings and often had plants growing around the entrance, unlike the ones in his dream, which were completely square. They were smooth and cold like the large noisy creatures, although their surfaces did not shine in the same way.

He lay down again and tried to sleep. The moon had risen and was shining through a break in the trees. It illuminated the little clearing in which he lay, its rays falling on and silhouetting a small bat as it circled silently backwards and forwards through the air, its senses guiding it infallibly through the trees. As he watched, his eyelids gradually became heavy and he fell into a deep, untroubled sleep.

When he opened his eyes again the sun had already risen. The birds had finished their early morning serenade and were busy foraging for food amongst the trees. As he rose, he realised that he too was hungry, famished in fact, as he had eaten nothing since the morning before. Time to find something good to eat! As he walked, he thought about what he would like most. A nice, juicy piece of fruit, or perhaps a handful of nuts, and then there were also berries… But yes, what he would *really* like was some honey, and then, there in front of him, nestling in a hole in a large tree, was a hive. He approached the hive cautiously and asked the bees respectfully if he might share some of their honey. The bees swarmed out of the hive, and for a moment they hovered before him, hanging suspended in mid air, looking for all the world like a mirror image of himself made completely out of bees. Then the shape melted away, and the bees flew off in a hundred different directions to spend the day collecting pollen, and he knew that he had their permission to take some honey.

He climbed the tree and thrust his hand deep into the hole and felt around gently, because he did not want to destroy what the bees had worked so hard to build. Then, when he felt the honeycomb beneath his fingers, he grasped a piece and pulled it out. Oh, how sweet and delicious it was! This really was his favourite food. When he had licked the last of the sticky substance from his fingers, he looked around for a tree that bore nuts. A little something to finish off with, he thought. Ah yes, there was a tree heavy with nuts, growing just beside the stream. His heart filled with gratitude and happiness as he splashed around in the stream, washing the last vestiges of stickiness from his hands and face. How good life was! Truly he wanted for nothing.

Chapter 2

The grey rocks that formed the coastline created a jagged silhouette against the fading light of the ageing day. The sea lapped lazily against them, leaving an oily trace wherever it touched, its greasy tendrils sucking and guzzling at the little inlets where it became trapped as it swirled and boiled like tar in a cauldron.

The cliffs formed a forbidding boundary to the land that lay beyond: barren and for the most part lifeless. Only the occasional tree remained, twisted and misshapen by its struggle for survival. Roots penetrating far down into the damaged soil in a desperate attempt to find nourishment deeper within the earth. They provided shelter for the few remaining creatures which scraped an existence from the damaged landscape. Pools of slimy green water dotted the desolate ground, bubbles of toxic gas constantly rising to the surface, where they burst with a loud popping sound, releasing the gas which fizzed and hissed as it rose into the air.

Thick, smokey clouds turned every day into perpetual dusk, as the sun could not penetrate the swirling fog. Hardly a ray of its light-giving warmth found a path through the gloom to the surface of this desolate place.

The wind prowled unchecked across the barren ground, whining and moaning as it whipped the poisonous pools into a frenzy, releasing lumps of strangely coloured foam which launched themselves crazily into the damp, grey air. Drinkable water was hard to find, so the rain, when it came, was always a welcome sight.

Huddled together in small groups, clinging to the lifeless ground like large, ramshackle limpets, were the huts fashioned from the wreckage of the past, which were home to the few remaining human beings left in this ravaged land. This small band of survivors eked out an existence here on the cliff tops, foraging for nuts hidden below the surface of the poisonous ground and occasionally trapping a few of the small animals that shared the ruined remains of their once beautiful world.

Eira sat staring lazily out to sea, dimly aware of the sound of her father's voice, which seemed to be receding further and further away. He was telling a small group of the younger villagers stories of the Before Times, when the Before People had dwelt here, and of how they had ruined the land. They sat, spellbound, listening to his words, gasping in horror, amazement and wonder at the images he created with his vivid descriptions of animals, birds, and people. She had heard these stories many times before, and they always filled her with a deep sadness and longing to see the world as it had been before it was spoiled. She had heard how the land had been green and beautiful, teaming with animals, birds, and fish, the ground covered in huge trees and richly scented plants. The people grew food in the fertile soil and picked fruit from the trees. Fresh, clear water cascaded down from the mountains and bubbled up in springs from under the ground.

The sea was a clear azure blue, and you could, so the storytellers said, see right to the bottom, where a myriad of brightly coloured fishes darted between the gently waving stems of a thousand different types of plants and corals. Larger fish swam and called to each other, their songs sending a ghostly echo through the waters. Yes, the sea too was beautiful.

The thought of all that had been lost caused her heart to ache with longing, and the more she thought about it, the fainter the sound of her father's voice became, until she could hear him no longer. For a while she drifted, as if in a dream. Indeed she must be dreaming, as the sea had turned a deep sapphire blue, reflecting the colour of the sky! The sky was blue! Fluffy white clouds drifted by and, yes, birds sailed on the wind, spreading their wings and riding the sea breezes. Clear, white spray splashed against the rocks and showered her face. She laughed, licking her lips and tasting the salt. How could this be?

For a while she stood looking out to sea, watching the birds, listening to their cries and breathing deeply of the clean, salt-laden air. How good it all was. Her heart raced and her spirits soared. She had no idea how she had got here. All she knew was that she wanted to stay forever! How different it was from her own home, although she recognised the rugged pattern of the rocks and guessed that she must be in the same place. But that place had been utterly transformed.

The sun was warm against her face, and she held out her arms to feel its comforting heat. She wanted to bathe her whole body in its beautiful, yellow light. Where she came from the sun was barely visible, only glimpsed dimly through a grey haze. Mist covered the ground most of the time, making the atmosphere damp and chill. She had never felt such warmth before, and it filled her with joy. Smiling to herself, she began to explore, walking inland away from the rocky coastline and the wheeling birds.

As she walked, the ground became soft beneath her feet. She could no longer feel the sharp hardness of the rocks. It yielded slightly as she trod upon it, tickling the soles of her feet and springing up under her weight. Surprised, she looked down and gasped. The ground was green, green with a thousand—no, a million—individual blades of grass all growing so closely together that they formed a shimmering emerald carpet for her to walk on. As she looked down in wonder at the grass, she saw, nestling between the blades, little splashes of colour. White, yellow, blue, and purple. Her father had taught her how to recognise and name the colours, for she had only seen them in an old manuscript that he kept hidden. It was part of the Wisdom that only the Knowers had access to, and her father said she was to inherit this knowledge from him. She would succeed him as their peoples' Knower. Gently, she bent down and picked one of the delicate little flowers and held it to her nose. It smelt faintly of something sweet and fragrant. Carefully, she wrapped it in a corner of her skirt. She would take it home and show her father. It would please him she was sure, and perhaps he would tell her some more about the Before Times. She longed to hear these stories again and again, and she would often beg her father to tell them, as she and her friends sat listening, entranced by his descriptions of forests, rivers, fields, and animals.

For a long time she wandered along the grassy cliff tops, revelling in the warmth and light, but after a while she grew tired and decided to rest a little before returning to the beach. There was no sign of her village nor any of her people. The place seemed deserted and she began to feel a little uneasy, but despite her feelings of unease the gentle warmth and beauty was so inviting that she sat down, and resting her back against a warm rock, lulled by the sound of bees gathering pollen from the little flowers at her feet, her eyes began to close and she was soon asleep.

As she slept, she dreamt that she wandered further from the beach and into a forest of huge trees, which were so tall that she could hardly make out their top branches. Shafts of sunlight pierced the canopy of leaves overhead and fell in little patches of dappled light on the ground in front of her. She stretched out her hand and could feel the warmth of the sunlight on her palm. Beneath her feet the ground gave slightly, gently snapping and crunching as she walked and giving off a faint, spicy smell.

Dreamily, she crept softly between the great trunks. But then she saw something moving out of the corner of her eye. Was someone following her? Peering through the dimly lit woodland, she thought she saw the figure of a man strolling through the trees. He seemed to be unaware of her presence and appeared to be absorbed in something, but she could not see what it was. Perhaps he was from her village, and he would be able to help her find her way back there. She quickened her pace in an attempt to catch up with him, but the faster she walked the further away he seemed to get. Suddenly, feeling very alone, she called out to him.

'Please, please wait. My name is Eira and I'm lost. Please will you help me?'

She thought that for a moment the figure paused and turned, but she could not be sure, as by this time he was almost out of sight, and then he vanished between the trees, and she was alone again.

Desolation flooded her whole being. She had never felt so alone before, and she cried out in desperation. Perhaps, if she called loudly enough, he would hear her and come back. But the only reply to her calls was the faint sound of woodland birds in the great forest. Her legs gave way beneath her, and dropping to her knees she put her head in her hands and wept.

Feeling a gentle touch on her head, she looked up into the kindly face of her father. She stared around her wildly. The forest, the grass, the birds, the blue sky and warm sunshine had all vanished, and she was back in her own village, her father standing over her with a look of concern on his face.

'Eira, my dear,' he said quietly, 'are you all right? You fell asleep and we could not wake you. We were so worried. You have slept for one whole day and night.'

'Yes, thank you, Father, I am all right now,' she replied shakily. 'I dreamt that I saw the sun and the blue sky. The ground was covered in flowers and grass. Birds called and flew in the air. Then I entered a great forest and saw a man in the distance. I called out to him, but he did not hear me, and I felt so lonely, so dreadfully lonely that I could not bear it, and then I was back here.'

If Eira had looked up at that moment, she would have seen a look of amazement, shock, and then awe on her father's face. He was remembering the words of the Prophecy. Could this be? he asked himself. Could his child really be the Chosen One? Had he fathered the One who would see the end of this dark time and a return of light to the world? Would she see the sun in all its glory again, feel its warmth on her face? She had seen the lone figure in the forest, had dreamt of how the world used to be in the Before Times. It could only mean one thing. But there had been no other signs. She, the Prophecy said, would not find him until *green-leafed tree and snow-clad hill stand together*. But when they were united there would be a new beginning, and all would be made whole once more.

Blissfully unaware of her father's consternation, Eira was thinking of the figure she had seen in the great forest and puzzling over her dream. It had all seemed so real, not like a dream at all. She was sure that she had really been there, felt the grass beneath her feet, heard the birds singing, and smelt the sweet, spicy smell of the trees. Then with a sudden thrill of excitement, she remembered the flower that she had picked on the cliffs. If it was still in her skirt, then she would know for certain that it had all been real, and she had not dreamt it after all. Carefully, she searched for the little corner of material near the hem where she had tied the flower, and there it was! Trembling with excitement, she carefully undid the knot and, scarcely daring to look, opened its folds. Out fell a small, purple flower, its petals crushed and broken, but unmistakably a flower. She gasped. What could this mean? How was this possible? Where had she been, and how had she got there?

Quickly she picked up the flower, eager to show it to her father, but he had already seen it and was staring at it open-mouthed.

'Where did you get this child?' he asked, trying to disguise the astonishment in his voice.

'I, I don't know,' stammered Eira. 'I dreamt that I picked it on the cliff top and put it in the fold of my skirt, but when I woke up it was still there. So it can't have been a dream, Father, can it? It must have been real?'

Adil looked at his daughter's puzzled face and felt a sudden pang of tenderness for her. Poor Eira, she knows nothing of her destiny, but she hears the Call, and it pulls on her heart so. My poor child, it is a heavy burden to carry for one so young. But although the journey ahead of her may be long and difficult, its end will bring a happiness beyond imagining to her and countless others. For the time being, he would say nothing to Eira. First he must be certain that she was indeed the Chosen One. He would make the journey to the Nuntius and read the Prophecy with Darius, his friend, wisest and oldest of all the Knowers.

Chapter 3

The following day, Eira was woken by the sound of voices. Her mother and father were talking in low, earnest tones. Her father was saying, 'I don't think it is wise to tell Eira why I have gone to see the Nuntius, not yet anyway. If his answer is as I suspect, I will explain everything to her when I return.'

'That's not going to be easy, Adil. You know how curious she is; she's bound to ask,' her mother replied. 'Surely it won't hurt for her to know. If, as you suspect, she is the Chosen One, then she has the *right* to know, and besides, I can talk to her and prepare the way for what you have to say when you return.'

Adil was silent for a moment. Of course, Bethan was right. There was no real justification for keeping the reason for his visit to Darius a secret. After all, if the Great Guardian had entrusted Eira with this extraordinary task, she surely needed no cosseting from her parents, or anyone else for that matter.

He nodded and, kissing his wife lovingly on the cheek, said, 'You are right. What would I do without your wisdom and insight? I leave all in your more-than-capable hands.' Taking up his staff and pack, he strode out onto the path which led up the cliffs from the beach and was soon out of sight.

Eira pulled the blanket up over her head and pretended to be asleep. She did not want her mother to know that she had heard their conversation, but her mind was racing. What could her father have meant? They couldn't possibly have been talking about her, could they? And what was her father going to ask the Nuntius? She knew vaguely from things he had said that the Nuntius was a very wise man, who had authority over all the Knowers, and that when she reached a certain point in her studies it was to him that she would be taken to learn the Greater Secrets and the Prophecy, before she could become a fully fledged Knower herself.

She must have fallen asleep again, because the next thing she heard was her mother calling her name. 'Eira, get up child, the sun has already risen, and I need your help this morning. We must go foraging for ground nuts.'

Sleepily, she dressed and ate the morsel of food that her mother offered her. Then picking up the gathering baskets, they joined the other villagers on their way to the cliff tops to forage for the small, green, nut-like fruits which grew just below the surface of the thin layer of soil which covered the dark, craggy rocks of the coast.

All that day they worked, kneeling on the cold, hard ground, working their way forwards inch by inch. As the fruits grew below the surface, it was necessary to dig through the thin soil in order to find them. A foul smelling mist swirled around them as they worked, making them cough, as the bitterness of it stung the backs of their throats. Their hair and clothing were soaked with its dampness, and the putrid stench clung to their skin. Her father and the other Knowers said that the Before People had caused the air to smell like this because they had poisoned the ground with things they called chemicals. These potions had supposedly been made for the good of the people, but they had only caused evil in the end.

As she worked, Eira thought about her dream. She pictured the blue sky and the green grass, and the elusive man she had seen in the distance amongst the trees. When she thought of this beautiful world, she forgot about the mist and the pain in her knees. Slowly her basket was filling up with ground nuts, and when it was full, she and her mother could go home. Then they would all sit around the fire until late, telling stories. She loved to listen to the storytellers, and she particularly liked it when her father, or one of the other Knowers, talked of the Before Times.

* * *

Adil set a brisk pace up the cliff path. He hoped to reach the home of the Nuntius by dusk, but the Sanctuary lay a great distance from here. He must make haste. It was not wise to be out after dark, as strange things stalked the shadows at night. Darius, the Nuntius, head of all the Knowers in the Lived-in-Lands, was an old and dear friend. They had known one another since boyhood and had studied the Greater Secrets and the Transmission of the Prophecy together. They understood each other well, and he felt sure Darius would know for certain if his daughter was indeed the Chosen One. He trusted his judgement implicitly.

The path snaked its way up the cliff, cutting between the dark, oily rocks. Strange, angular plants grew from cracks in their high walls. They were completely rigid, unmoved by any wind that might blow. Even the gales that buffeted the coast from time to time did not move them, for they were made from a strange organic crystal, which formed itself into these odd, plant-like structures, their smooth, hard surfaces glittering in the poor light.

Soon the path levelled out, and he began to make his way inland away from the grey, restless sea. The ground was bare, covered by a thin layer of dusty soil, blanketed by the ever-present mist, which clung wetly to his ankles. Ahead, he could see the great mounds of rubble which marked his way, and then he heard the first telltale crunching sounds, and he knew he had reached the Plain of the Dead. This vast area, so the legends said, had once been a great city in the Before Times, and it was here that untold numbers of the Before People had perished. Their bodies still lay upon the ground, unburied and unmourned. The crunching sound he could hear was the sound of their bones beneath his feet.

With a shudder he pressed on; he could not let the

feeling of this place unnerve him. The wind had got up and it whipped his cloak tightly around his body. Sighing and stirring up the ground, it rattled and whispered over the great plain, filling him with an almost overwhelming sense of horror and despair. He *must* continue; there was nothing here to be feared. It was only the wind and the bones of the long dead; nothing that could harm him, he told himself firmly. Quietly, he repeated to himself over and over the words of the Prophecy:

When green-leafed tree and snow-clad hill stand together,
She will awaken and know Herself.
Then shall the Two who wander alone be joined and
*   become One.*
The Circle will complete itself and all will be made whole
*   again.*
Spring will return to the Lived-in-Lands.

The power in the words of the Prophecy seemed to calm him and, he felt, afford him some protection from the oppressive atmosphere of this place. It would take him at least an hour to cross the Plain of the Dead, and the sun was already well past its zenith. He must hurry. Fortunately, the mist hid from his nervous gaze the grizzly sight of what covered the ground on which he must walk.

At last he saw, looming through the haze, the sight which he had been longing to see for the last few hours. The flat plain ended abruptly in a great wall of rock, through the middle of which ran a great tunnel. The rock was a strange red colour and appeared to be formed in small squares. He knew from the Teachings that it had been built by the Before People, and that great metal beasts had run through the huge tunnel, carrying hundreds of people in their bellies. Now it was just a dark, empty passage through the great wall. This was the most difficult part of his journey, for the tunnel was several spans in length. It would take some time to pass through, and he had no light to aid him. He would have to traverse its length in pitch darkness. This in itself was not too difficult, as it was a simple matter to run his hand along the wall as he passed through. It was the possibility of meeting one of the night stalkers, or Noctu, as the Knowers called them, who were said to inhabit places such as this, which filled him with dread.

These creatures lived in the dark places and only came out into the open at night. They were, it was said, the misshapen relics of some hideous experiments which the Before People had carried out. The Before People had taken the minute strands of life, which hold the matrix of a species, and mixed them, man and animal together. What they produced was a walking horror, as afraid of itself as it was of its makers. These poor creatures were said to have survived the destruction that the Before People wrought upon themselves, and they still lurked in the shadowy places of the Lived-in-Lands, bent on revenge. And if you were unfortunate enough to come upon one of them, it was unlikely that you would live to tell the tale. But he must continue, and so taking a deep breath and pausing only long enough to listen for sounds in the tunnel, he plunged into the inky blackness.

Keeping one hand firmly in contact with the smooth wall, he picked his way as quietly and quickly as he could through the passage. The sound of dripping water echoed eerily in the stillness, and the noise of his own feet shuffling on the stony floor was amplified so that it seemed to create such a din that he thought he would scream with the loudness of it. He had no wish to disturb anything which might be lurking here. The shadows seemed to take shape and follow him, as his eyes strained for the slightest pin-prick of light, but there was none. He fancied he could hear something breathing. Frozen with terror, he strained to listen for the dreaded dragging footsteps, but there were none, and he realised with a flood of relief that the breathing was his own. Gulping down a sense of panic, he continued, and then to his delight he glimpsed the faintest chink of light and smelt the now almost welcome stench of the ever present mist. He was nearly through.

Stumbling out of the tunnel into what was left of the daylight, he gasped with relief, and hastened to put some distance between himself and the opening into that dark and uncertain world. Now the rest of the way was easy. The ground was even, almost flat, and in the distance he caught sight of his goal at last. The great stone circle, sacred meeting place of all the Knowers in the Lived-in-Lands, and home to the Great Nuntius. Dimly through the shrouded sky, he could see that the sun was beginning its slow descent, and would soon be lost below the horizon. The ancient stones, put there so long ago that even the Before People had no knowledge or memory of the architects, framed the dim light of the setting sun, lit by its faint, rosy glow.

He increased his pace, eager to complete his journey and see his old friend Darius again. They would sit by the fire and exchange news and stories over a pipe or two, and he smiled with pleasure at the prospect. When he was about two hundred paces from the outermost circle of stones, a figure detached itself from beside one of the great standing stones and walked towards him. It was a young man, dressed in the ceremonial robes of the Guardians of the Sacred Circle. Those judged to have the right abilities were sent here to study the Wisdom, and all hoped one day to become Knowers. They had all pledged themselves to serve the Nuntius for a year and a day. At the end of that time they could choose to remain as permanent servants of the Prophecy, or they could return to their homes and continue their studies in preparation for their initiation into the full understanding of the Wisdom.

'Halt, stranger,' the young man called, lifting his outstretched arm and barring Adil's way with his staff. 'What business have you here?' he continued.

Adil, bowing low, said, 'Greetings, respected Guardian. I have come to consult the Great Nuntius on a matter of the utmost importance. It concerns the Prophecy. I am known to him as the Knower Adil from the Grey Coast.'

The Guardian inclined his head. The Guardians bowed to no one except the Great Nuntius. Lowering his staff, he instructed Adil to remain where he was. Then turning swiftly on his heel, he vanished between the stones.

Adil waited for the Guardian to return. He was confident that Darius would see him, but protocol and ceremony had to be observed. He must be patient. At home he was used to being respected and obeyed by the whole community, but here he was just another Knower seeking audience from his guide and teacher. He must wait. But he did not have to wait long, for the Guardian quickly returned, carrying a warm fur cloak, which he placed around Adil's shoulders with a smile, and said, 'Darius greets his old friend and bids you join him by the fire. You must be tired and hungry after your long journey.'

Together they walked between the great stones into the centre of the circle, where several figures sat around a blazing fire. One of the men stood up a little stiffly and walked slowly towards the pair. The firelight shone on the old man's face, and he saw that it was Darius. How he has aged, Adil thought to himself, as he greeted his old friend.

With outstretched arms, Darius clasped the younger man's hands and drew him towards the fire. 'Adil, my dear, dear friend, how glad I am to see you after all this time. Come and sit by the fire; warm yourself.'

Turning to the young Guardian he said, 'Bring food and drink for the respected Knower. He has travelled far today and is weary.'

The Guardian bowed low and retreated, returning a few moments later with a steaming bowl of broth and some roasted ground nuts, which Adil accepted eagerly. He was famished.

When he had eaten his fill, Darius turned to him and asked, 'You have travelled a long and dangerous road. No one undertakes such a journey except with great need. What do you have to tell me?'

Adil was silent for a moment, and then he began to recount Eira's dream and the appearance of the purple flower. Darius listened to the whole story without saying a word, all the while drawing gently on his pipe. When Adil had finished he nodded thoughtfully. Then looking up he said, 'This is important news, and, if she is indeed the Chosen One, it is cause for great joy. But first we must be sure. I shall reflect on what you have told me, and you must rest now. In the morning we shall read the Prophecy and consult the Signs together, for we must be absolutely sure of our ground before we speak of this to anyone else and, in particular, to Eira herself. She will need all the help we can give her, as the transition will be a testing time for her.'

The two men parted and Adil made himself comfortable by the fire. Wrapping his cloak around himself, he settled down to sleep. Darius made his way to the small stone temple, where the records of the Before People and the sacred writings of the Prophecy were kept. He must spend some time considering what Adil had told him. They would meet again at first light.

Chapter 4

The first thin rays of sunlight pierced the grey gloom of the new day. The fire had burned down and was now just a pile of glowing red hot embers. Adil stirred and looked about him. His companions around the fire were already up and busying themselves with the first tasks of the morning. Between the main standing stones he glimpsed a figure with outstretched arms, holding a long staff. He knew that the Guardian was performing the Ceremony of Greeting, which was done at the beginning of each new day to welcome the sun and the prospect of new life and renewal. Since the end of the Great Disaster, when a small band of survivors struggled to live in their ruined world, this ceremony had been performed to show gratitude for what they had, in the hope that the land would in time be healed and become fruitful once more.

Usually the ceremony would be performed by the

Great Nuntius, but this morning, although the man had his back to him, Adil could see that it was not Darius standing there between the great stones. The man lowered his staff, bowed, turned, and walked towards him. He could see that the Guardian was not a young man. He must be one of those who had taken the Great Oath to remain here and guard the Nuntius and the Prophecy, Adil thought to himself.

'Good morning, respected Guardian,' Adil said, bowing. 'Where might I find the Great Nuntius, Darius? We have much to discuss this morning.'

The man smiled, and pointed in the direction of the little stone temple. 'You will find him in the temple, where he has been all night. He awaits you and bids you break the fast with him.'

Adil thanked the Guardian, and made his way to the temple. Bending low to enter the sacred building, for the doorway was small, he found Darius sitting bent over a large book, its pages worn and discoloured with age. He was deeply engrossed, pouring over the ancient text, repeating the words before him in a soft whisper, as he strained to read the faded script. At first he did not hear Adil enter, but then, as he approached, Darius raised his head and greeted his old friend, but there was a faraway look in his eyes. It was a look that Adil had seen only once before, in the eyes of his daughter, Eira, when she had recounted her dream of the great forest, the elusive man, and his beautiful green world.

Reverently, Darius closed the old book to reveal its cover. Bound in green leather, it bore a strange symbol which Adil had never seen before. Not even when he had been initiated into the Wisdom and shown the words of the Prophecy had he seen this thing. Painted in colours of scintillating brightness was a curious creature, a dragon or a huge snake, he thought to himself. It held its tail in its mouth. Its eyes glittered a piercing emerald green, and they had a most disquieting effect upon him. Try as he might, he could not take his eyes off them, and when he did so they seemed to follow him with their gaze. The creature seemed to be alive!

Taking a step backwards, he gasped. Darius eyed him keenly.

'Ah, the Uroboros has that effect on those who have never seen it before,' he said, smiling enigmatically. 'I know what you are thinking, and the answer is indeed yes, the creature is alive, in a sense. What you see is just an image, a pictorial representation of a force, powerful beyond anything we could possibly imagine. But, because that force is so immense, it infuses this symbol with some of its power. This picture is our link to the eternal force of renewal.'

As Darius spoke, Adil thought he detected a movement in the creature's body, and then it seemed to be sliding through space at tremendous speed. Faster and faster it went, until he could no longer see it clearly, for it was just a blur. Somehow he could not take his eyes off it; he was compelled to witness the creature's headlong dash through space and time. Nausea overwhelmed him, and then everything went black.

* * *

Slowly, he raised his head and looked about him. At first he thought that he was in the little stone temple, and that Darius must have carried him to the soft and comfortable couch on which he seemed to be resting. Then, as his vision cleared, he saw that he was outside, and, looking down with a start of amazement, realised that the soft couch was in fact a thick patch of grass. The sun was rising and filled the clear sky with a glow the colour of rubies. Streaks of pink and yellow flashed across its shimmering brightness, and the air smelt fresh and sweet. He lay back on his soft bed of grass, transfixed by the sheer beauty around him.

Leaping to his feet, he ran with arms outstretched, just for the sheer pleasure of it. He felt light; all his cares had vanished. In the distance he saw a winding stream, which danced and chattered its way towards a great forest. Making his way over to the stream, he knelt and drank deeply of the cool, refreshing water. As he did so, he caught sight of his reflection. Gasping, he fell backwards onto the grassy bank feeling his face with his hands. Cautiously he peeped into the water again, and yes, there was no mistake: he had the face of a young man again. Looking down at his hands and body, he saw, not the body of a middle-aged man who had spent most of his life scavenging for morsels of food to stay alive, but a strong, well-muscled, well-nourished young man.

This was indeed the strangest thing, he thought. *How can this be? Perhaps I should go to the forest, and maybe I will meet Eira's elusive man, for surely this is the place that she described in her dream.* Rising to his feet he set off in the direction of the great wood. He found himself running effortlessly, mile after mile. He jogged tirelessly towards the great trees, but they never seemed to get any closer. Finally as the sun climbed high in the sky, he stopped near a small group of bushes, and, seeing they bore a kind of fruit, picked a handful and ate his fill. As he sat enjoying their juicy sweetness and the warmth of the sun on his face, it occurred to him that he was not meant to reach the forest or to meet its mysterious inhabitant, at least not yet, and he smiled. That was for his daughter, Eira, of course.

Then why am I here? he wondered. As if in answer to his silent question he heard a voice calling his name, a voice so soft that it sounded like the sighing of the wind in the trees. There was something strangely familiar about it, but when he thought about it later he could not say what it was.

'Adil. Adil, listen to what I have to say.'

Jumping to his feet, Adil looked about him but could not see the owner of the voice. 'Where are you? Come out so that I can see you,' he called, but there was no answer.

Presently the voice continued, 'Do you know why you have been brought here?'

'No', Adil replied uncertainly. 'But this is clearly a place of great beauty and renewal, and I am on a quest to seek answers to my daughter's vision. Could it be that I have been shown this place so that I might find the guidance I seek here?'

'Your heart guides you well, Adil of the Grey Coast,' the voice replied. 'It is not for you to reach the forest, but having seen this place, you must return home to your daughter and give her this Message of

Hope. When she hears these words, she will take heart and have the power to fulfil her destiny.'

Trembling, Adil asked, 'What words must I speak to Eira, Greatest of all the Nuntii?'

'The words are imprinted on your heart, and you will speak them when the time is right,' the voice replied.

'But how will I know?' Adil called. But there was only silence and the distant sound of water splashing on the rocks in the little brook. The light was fading now, and, suddenly feeling very tired, he looked around for a comfortable place to spend the night. He had no idea how long he was to remain in this place, but for now he must sleep, and then who knows what the new day would bring. Of one thing he was sure: he would see his daughter again soon, as the voice had commanded him to convey a message to her, and so he was reassured. With the words of the mysterious voice still echoing in his head, he curled up under the fruit bushes on a patch of soft moss and was soon asleep.

'Adil, Adil, are you all right?' An anxious voice, which seemed to come from a great distance away, was calling him, drifting towards him as he floated on a sea of blackness. Opening his eyes slowly, Adil saw Darius's concerned face swim into view. Sitting bolt upright, he stared wildly about him. The little stream, the fruit bushes, the soft green grass and the great forest, all had disappeared, and he was back in the little stone temple with Darius bending over him.

'How long have I been asleep?' Adil asked, confused, for the grey morning light was visible through a small window set high in the wall, and it had been nightfall when he had lain down to sleep by the brook.

'My dear friend, you were unconscious, not sleeping, but only for a few moments. The Uroboros can have a strange effect on those who see it for the first time, and it can bring dreams and visions to the worthy.'

Adil nodded, hesitating for a moment, for he did not want Darius to think him mad, before recounting his vision of the beautiful green world, the great forest, and the invisible messenger.

When he had finished, Darius, who had been sitting silently the whole time with his head slightly bowed, looked up and straight into the eyes of his friend. 'Adil, Knower of the Grey Coast, honoured guest, you have been in the Presence of the Great Guardian, Greatest Knower of them all. *The One* who presides over time itself. Ignore the message you were given at your peril. If you do, the consequences not only for yourself but for all of us will be dire. The One did not show Itself to you because no mortal can look upon such great power and live. The sight of It would have destroyed you in an instant.'

Adil felt light-headed and slumped back in his chair. This was indeed a great responsibility for a simple man like himself to carry, he thought. What if he was unable to speak the words in his heart? What would happen to him, to Eira, to them all?

Darius, as if hearing his friend's thoughts, answered, 'Do not be afraid, Adil; the Great Guardian speaks only to those whose intentions are pure. None are ever punished simply because they may appear to fail, for who are we to say what is success and what is failure? Only the Wisdom can know such things. Now you must prepare yourself for the return journey to your village. There is no time to waste, as the sun is already up and you do not want to be on the road after nightfall.'

His pack filled with what little food the community of Guardians could spare, Adil took leave of his friend. Darius embraced him and pressed something cold and hard into his hand.

'Take this with my blessing; it may help you on the road. There are dark times ahead before we see the clear light of the sun again.'

Looking down, Adil opened his hand to reveal a miniature version of the strange creature which he had seen on the cover of the old book in the temple. It was fashioned from a curious metal which glowed like the sun and seemed to take warmth from his hand. Its eyes were inset with green stones which sparkled and flashed in the poor light. It was threaded onto a thin chain made of the same metal, and Darius gestured for him to put it around his neck.

'May the Great Guardian watch over you and keep you safe. I will watch the horizon for the rising of the new sun. Listen to your heart, and all will be well.'

Adil struggled to find words of thanks, but his heart was so full that no words would come, and he clutched his friend's hand, tears springing up in his eyes. Darius's eyes too were wet with tears, and, gesturing with his hand, he pointed out the path that would take the traveller away from the stone circle, down the hill, and out across open ground towards the great wall and its dark, forbidding tunnel.

* * *

For several miles Adil walked not daring to look back, for there lay safety and friendship. He had a long and dangerous journey ahead, and the huge responsibility of what he must reveal to Eira weighed heavily upon him. Setting his face resolutely in the direction of the tunnel and the Plain of the Dead, he trudged on.

The day was unusually warm and the mist seemed a little thinner than usual. Swirling around his ankles in wispy strands, it smelt a little sweeter today, he thought, but that was surely just his imagination. Somewhere to his left, he heard a sharp, rattling sound, and turning towards the noise he spotted a small, snake-like creature with two heads. It skittered and slithered across the stony ground, hissing at him when he got too close. But it appeared to mean him no harm, and so the two let each other be, and he continued on his journey. It puzzled him though, as he had never seen any living thing out here. The ground was devoid of any vegetation, although there were probably ground nuts below the surface. So what did the creature feed on? he wondered.

He reached the tunnel just after midday, and as there was plenty of daylight left he decided to break his journey and eat a little of the food that the Guardians had given him. With his back leaning against the tunnel wall, he sat and feasted on ground nuts. As he rested there, the little snake appeared as if from nowhere and slithered right up to his foot, where it rested, seeming to watch him, tasting the air with its two forked tongues. On an impulse he tossed one of the ground nuts in the creature's direction, and to his surprise it opened its two mouths, the lucky mouth catching and devouring the tasty morsel with relish. Deciding that the other mouth should also have a treat, he tossed the snake a second nut, which the other head caught with ease. Laughing, he held out his hand to the tiny reptile, but it slithered away to a safe distance and coiled itself around a small rock, watching him with its two pairs of black, beady eyes.

Rising wearily to his feet, he prepared to continue his journey and enter the tunnel. With his left hand brushing the wall as he went he set off, keeping up as brisk a pace as he could manage. The damp stones seemed slimy underfoot, and his feet slipped and slithered as he walked. Strange: he did not remember it being so slippery on the outward journey. But perhaps there had been some rain in his absence, which had caused the algae to bloom. The Before People had polluted the water so badly that a strange type of algae had appeared. It grew in such vast quantities that it could clog a whole river in a matter of days and absorb so much of the water that nothing else could survive. But here there was no river, so it covered the ground like a slimy, evil-smelling blanket.

Strange though: he had not remembered the algae smelling so distasteful before. An odour like that of rotting corpses arose from beneath his feet. It was so foul that it made him retch and gasp for breath. He was now well into the tunnel, and the last chink of daylight had vanished behind him. As he struggled to keep his balance on the slippery surface, he became aware of a faint sound off to his right. It sounded like breathing: heavy, laboured breathing. He stopped for a moment and held his breath, thinking that it was the sound of his own breath echoing through the tunnel, but to his horror the sound continued. A rising sense of panic gripped him, but he could not run. It was far too treacherous under foot. He must keep his head as well as his footing!

Adil began to move cautiously along the tunnel again, trying to make as little noise as possible in the hope that whatever was nearby was not aware of his presence and he could put some distance between it and him before it heard him. Every step was like walking on thin ice, waiting for it to crack under his weight, waiting for—he dared not think what. The possibilities were too horrible to contemplate. He recalled again the stories of the creatures that stalked the dark places filled with hatred for mankind. Betrayed by the Before People who had made them, then abandoned them, leaving them to die, hated and feared by the very people who had brought them into existence.

Slap, slap, slap: the wet, dragging sound echoed through the tunnel with terrifying proximity. Adil suppressed a scream of terror. Sweat trickled down his face, dripping into his eyes, making them sting. To his horror the sound was coming from in front of him now, blocking his escape route. He was done for, and he felt the dreadful lead weight of inevitability clamp down on his shoulders. His fate was to die here in this tunnel, killed by some unmentionable horror. His wife and daughter would watch hopefully for his return day after day, until at last they would lose hope and mourn his loss. He would never be able to tell Eira what he had seen and heard in the stone circle.

Suddenly, from behind him, he heard the now

familiar slithering rattle of the little two-headed snake. It had followed him into the tunnel! Looking down, he could just make out its tiny form in the inky blackness, its scales shining slightly in the slimy wetness of the tunnel floor. He bent down and was about to speak to the serpent, when something long and pink shot out of the darkness, wrapping itself around the wriggling snake, and then both were gone, and there was silence. He flattened himself against the tunnel wall, gripped by a growing sense of revulsion. There was no doubt now: one of the night stalkers was in the tunnel with him.

'Why are you so afraid, man beast?' The voice floated towards him out of the blackness. It sounded thin, as if the words it spoke were formed with difficulty; an alien language, spoken out of necessity. It sounded almost resentful.

'Who are you?' Adil's voice echoed around the damp walls of his prison and it sounded high, quavering, full of fear.

The other voice mocked him, 'Now who is afraid? Your kind have caused my people to live and die in fear for generations, and now it is your turn. How does it feel, man beast? Are you afraid to die? Perhaps you will wish that you were dead before the end. Perhaps you think that I will tear you limb from limb and consume your beating heart before your still-living eyes.'

'I wish you no harm.' Adil tried to suppress the sick fear which was rising in his throat. His heart was beating so fast that he was sure the creature could hear it. 'My people too struggle to survive in this ruined world. We are not responsible for your suffering. The

Before People made you. They grew arrogant and thought they could take the matrix of life itself and change it, but that is not for mankind to do. Surely their intentions were good in the beginning, but they grew increasingly ambitious in their plans, and life has a way of restoring its own balance, so their endeavours went horribly wrong, and you were born.' Adil drew a deep breath and continued, 'Will you not show yourself, so that we may talk face to face. Perhaps then we could begin to understand each other,' he added, his voice shaking with fear.

'Do you really think you can stand the sight of this ruined body?' the creature said.

'If you have the courage to reveal yourself, then the least I can do is honour that courage,' Adil replied.

'As you wish. But many of those who have looked on me have gone mad with terror.'

'I will take the risk. You are nothing more than a fellow creature after all. Let us go to the tunnel entrance; it is too dark for me to see you here.'

'So be it.' The creature's voice had lost its mocking tone and sounded almost wistful.

Slowly they made their way through the passage, Adil all the time keeping his left hand on the wall. Behind him came the shuffling, laboured breathing that was the walking horror waiting to reveal itself to him in the cold light of day. All too soon, a dim light appeared in the distance. Soon they would be out in the open. Would he be able to bear the sight of his companion? Or would one glance turn him mad, as it had said that it would.

Daylight surrounded him, and turning Adil looked

back at… nothing. The tunnel entrance was empty, and he stared back into a black void. The creature had gone. An overwhelming sense of relief swept over him, and he felt light-headed. His legs gave way under him and he sank to the ground with a sob. He did not know how long he lay there outside the tunnel, his eyes closed, listening to his pounding heart gradually resume its normal rhythm. He could not move, as his limbs felt like lead weights drained of all energy and purpose. The prospect of the creature re-emerging from the darkness did not enter his head. It was gone and would not return, of that he was sure.

Slowly, he became aware that he was icy cold and very hungry. What time of day was it? He must continue his journey for he needed to cross the Plain of the Dead before nightfall. There could be other night stalkers who would not be so quick to leave him in peace, as the poor wretch in the tunnel had done. The sun was on its downward path and had nearly reached the horizon. He must delay no longer. Quickly, he crammed a handful of ground nuts into his mouth, before rising stiffly to his feet, and stepping out onto the great open plain with its long dead inhabitants.

As he walked he thought about the creature in the tunnel. Its voice had sounded so human, and yet its speech so utterly unlike any man that he had ever heard. Full of hatred and laden with bitterness, why had it shown him mercy? For it could easily have killed him in the tunnel, or terrified him with the sight of it, and even then slaughtered him in the cold light of day; but it had not done so. He had trespassed in its world, but it would not enter his. For this he was truly grateful. Then, almost without realising what he was doing, his hand alighted upon the small metal amulet around his neck. The symbol of the Uroboros. To his amazement the creature's eyes were ablaze. Could it be that Darius's gift had saved him? That it had protected him from the horror in the darkness? He did not know. But the possibility filled him with a growing sense of the enormity of what was before him, and a sense of urgency pushed him on to greater speed. He must reach home tonight, for he could risk no more close shaves with death. He had been entrusted with a most extraordinary task, and he must not fail. Too much rested on his success.

Chapter 5

Her father had said that he would be away for three days. Why had he gone to visit Darius at the Stone Circle? It was a difficult and dangerous journey, only to be undertaken on matters of the greatest importance, such as when a new Knower was to be initiated. She was looking forward to the day when she would make that journey herself. In fact, she had been a little disappointed when her father had left her behind this time. Was she not old enough now? She had studied hard and knew the Prophecy backwards, and she knew by heart many of the stories of the Before Times, which every Knower of any standing must know. Why had he not taken her too? It must indeed be something very important to make her father leave and not share his secret with her. He always confided in her. But not this time, and it puzzled and upset Eira. Perhaps he was angry with her, but why? No, that could not be it;

she had done nothing to displease him. Oh well, she would just have to wait until he returned, and perhaps he would take her into his confidence then.

It was the day after her father's departure, and Eira was walking on the cliff tops alone, searching in the crevices between the rocks for a small plant which sometimes grew there. It was a kind of lichen, but at about this time of year it produced tiny saffron coloured flowers which, if you put them in your mouth, tasted deliciously sweet. They were so small that the sweetness lasted only a moment, but it was worth it. When she was free from her tasks at home and from her studies with her father, she would spend hours up here searching for the tasty treats.

Scrambling amongst the rocks, peering into every crevice, Eira lost track of time, until glancing up at the sky, she realised that the sun had begun to sink down below the horizon. It would soon be dusk, and then it would be difficult to see the path around the cliffs to the village. Tying her skirt tightly around her body to stop it from tripping her up, she began the rocky descent. It had rained the day before and the ground was slippery underfoot causing her to slip and slide as she made her way down the path. Small stones trickled and clicked after her. Like tiny ball bearings, they rolled beneath her feet, and before she realised what was happening she was careering down the path at breakneck speed, her arms flailing wildly as she struggled to keep her balance.

Flushed with alarm, she instinctively leaned backwards to check her mad dash downhill, but in doing so she lost her balance and fell, landing flat on her back, her head making contact with the hard ground with a resounding crack. For a brief moment the world before her eyes seemed to be full of brightly coloured stars and multicoloured patterns, then everything went black, and she lost consciousness.

* * *

A small bird was singing his heart out on a nearby tree branch, and the most heavenly smells hung in the still, warm air. Eira opened her eyes and put her hand up to feel the back of her head, where she felt sure there would be an enormous bump, but there was nothing, and she had no pain, no headache; in fact she felt wonderful! The ground on which she lay felt soft and warm, yielding gently beneath her questing hand. Looking down, she saw with delight that it was grass, and that she was surrounded by trees. Some of the trees had strange, brightly coloured objects hanging from them, and with a thrill of pleasure she realised that the objects must be fruit. Reaching up to one of the lower branches she picked a small, smooth, purple fruit and put it cautiously to her lips. Its fragrance encouraged her to take a bite, and as the taste of the sweet flesh exploded in her mouth she cried out in amazement. She had never tasted anything like this in her life before; it was delicious!

Looking around her, Eira sensed that she was back in the same place that she had dreamt of before, but this time she had awoken on the edge of the forest. Her first thought was of the mysterious figure she had seen here before. She hoped that she would see him again, and maybe this time she would succeed in attracting his attention. He might know the meaning of her dreams and why she was here. Realising that her time in the forest might be short, she lost no time in beginning her search. Jumping to her feet, she walked further into the denser part of the wood and began calling, 'Is there anybody there? Can you hear me? I am Eira, and I mean you no harm. Please, I need to talk to you.'

But there was no reply. Only the droning of insects and the calling of birds could be heard in the forest. Undeterred, she pushed on deeper and deeper amongst the great trees, until the light of the sun was almost completely blotted out by the dense foliage above her head.

* * *

Head bowed, he sat by a little pool watching the fish dart between the rocks. The water was crystal clear and he could see all the way to the bottom, where newts and all manner of small creatures were going confidently about their business, unhindered by doubts and questions. He was deep in thought, thinking about the creature he had seen in the wood the other day. He had only seen it in the far distance, but from what he had seen it had looked a little like him, only somehow different. It had long hair and was smaller, more delicate than him. He likened it to the deer that ran in the forest: soft, gentle and graceful. Whilst he compared himself to the stag that watched over the deer and called to them with his great voice echoing across the land. He did not know what caused him to make these comparisons, but it seemed to fit somehow.

He was sure that the creature had called out to him, and its call had sounded very like his thoughts, for he had never heard his own voice out loud, except when he imitated the calls of animals and birds. This puzzled him, for it must have been thinking out loud, and he did not know how this was possible.

Looking into the pool, he caught sight of his reflection, and began to wonder why there were no more of his kind. All the other animals had companions and mates. Every year they produced young ones, which they cared for until they too grew into adult creatures, who in their turn had young of their own. But he had never found such a companion for himself. He was alone. With a start, he realised that he had never questioned this state of affairs before, had never asked himself why he had no mate, and so he had never looked for one. All seemed to be right and as it should be, but somehow, since he had glimpsed the mysterious being through the trees, all that had changed and he felt restless and discontented. He must find this other self again, so that he could see his image standing before him, in the flesh, and not just a shimmering reflection in the water, shifting and moving with every ripple.

Rising thoughtfully to his feet, he began to walk slowly back through the forest, listening, searching for the other me, as he now called the mysterious creature. As he listened intently, hoping to hear those spoken thoughts again, he heard, carried faintly on a gentle breeze, the sound of a voice calling. It was calling him, he felt sure, and eagerly he began to run towards the sound. The voice was louder now, calling, 'Is there anybody there?'

'Yes! Yes, I am here,' he shouted. Gasping, he jumped, startled at the sound of his own voice calling. He had made a thought out loud. It had sounded like the other creature's thoughts, only louder, deeper somehow. More cautiously this time, he tried again. 'I want to see you, reflection of me.'

But no answer came. Frantically, he ran towards the place where he thought he had last heard the other voice, but there was nothing there except a woodpecker busily drilling for insects in an old, fallen tree trunk.

* * *

Startled, Eira stopped calling. She was sure that she heard something. Another voice answering her, a man's voice. Hastily she made her way in the direction the voice had come from, only to see a figure running through the trees some distance away. She waved frantically at him, but he did not seem to see her. 'I'm here, over here! This way!' she called, but he had passed out of sight. Dejectedly, she sat on the warm earth beneath a huge tree, tears of disappointment welling up in her eyes. Why had he not seen her? He had answered her call and was obviously trying to find her. She couldn't understand how they had missed each other this time. She felt a sudden dreadful emptiness. *I must find him*, she thought. A terrible sense of urgency gripped her, almost desperation. *I cannot give up now; we must meet. I know we are meant to meet.* She had never felt more certain of anything in her life before. Exhausted by her frantic search, she rested her head on the tree trunk and closed her eyes. Lulled by the sounds of the forest around her, she soon fell asleep.

* * *

'Oh, my head!' Eira groaned, as a sharp stab of pain jolted her awake. Slowly she sat up, taking in her surroundings. She was no longer sitting under the great tree in the forest but in the middle of the cliff path which led to her village, and she had an enormous lump on the back of her head. She sat for a while, dazed and confused. What was she doing here? Then, with a rush, it all came back to her. How she had been hurrying down the path and must have slipped and fallen, hitting her head as she fell, knocking herself unconscious. And it was then that she had found herself back in the forest. With a pang of longing and regret, she remembered seeing the mysterious man running through the trees, and that they had called to each other, but somehow, and this was the most puzzling thing of all, somehow they had been unable to reach each other.

It was now pitch dark, and the way down the cliff was treacherous, but she must get home. Her mother would be worried about her. Slowly, she rose to her feet, wincing as the pain in her head reminded her to be cautious. As she picked her way carefully down the path, her thoughts were full of her strange experiences in the great wood. Questions flooded her mind. How had she got there? It had all seemed so real. She had gone to sleep, as if she had already been awake, but clearly she had been unconscious all the time. Why had she and the stranger been unable to meet, seeming to drift apart like that? It was all very odd, and for the first time since her mysterious adventure had begun, she felt a little shiver of fear. Perhaps she was going mad, and none of this was real after all.

In the distance, she caught sight of a figure looking up the path. In the dim light she couldn't make out who it was, but she guessed that it was her mother, watching anxiously for her return.

'Eira, Eira, is that you? Are you all right?' the voice called.

'Yes, Mother, it's me. I'm sorry I'm late. I missed my footing and fell. I must have hit my head and passed out, because the last thing I remember is slipping on some loose stones. It was late, and I was hurrying to return home before it got dark. The next thing I knew I was waking up with this huge lump on my head.'

'Thank goodness, child! I was so worried about you,' her mother said breathlessly, hurrying to meet her, and looking searchingly at her daughter.

'I'm fine, Mother, really, but I had the strangest dream.' And as they made their way back to the village, she began to tell her mother about the forest and its elusive occupant.

Sitting by a roaring fire, sipping a bowl of hot broth, Eira finished her story. Her mother, who had listened in silence, eyed her daughter keenly and said: 'Eira my dear, this is indeed a most wondrous thing that you speak of, and I do not think you are going mad. But your father and I thought it best not to press you to talk about your experiences until he had consulted the Great Nuntius. One thing I can tell you though, is that he has gone to tell Darius about your dream. But we must be patient and wait to hear what Darius had to say,' she added firmly.

Bethan put a comforting arm around her daughter's shoulder and, hugging her lovingly, said gently: 'Rest now, and don't be afraid. There is nothing to fear, of that I am certain, only cause for great rejoicing.' Covering her daughter with a blanket, Bethan returned to sit by the fire, where she stayed long into the night, staring into the dying embers and occasionally looking over at the now sleeping form of her child. She had counselled Eira not to be afraid, but she was deeply troubled, as although she did not know what Darius would say to Adil, she felt with the instinct of a mother that there were testing times ahead for them all, and particularly for Eira.

The first thin rays of dawn found Bethan still sitting by the now cold embers of the fire. She had not been able to sleep at all that night and was stiff with cold. She had to stir herself. Eira should not see her like this; she must not know that she was worried. Slowly, as her hands were so cold and would not obey her, she lit the fire, blowing on the little spark to breathe life into it. Soon she had a roaring blaze going. Sighing with pleasure, she rubbed her hands to warm them, and then set a pot of water on the fire to boil. She would make some ground nut porridge for them this morning, a rare treat.

Eira awoke feeling much better. The pain in her head was gone, and the only reminder of her tumble down the cliff was a huge lump on the back of her head.

'Do you feel well enough to go foraging today?' Bethan asked.

'Yes, Mother, I'm fine now,' Eira replied smiling as she gulped her porridge down hungrily. 'It will help the time to pass more quickly until Father returns. I can't wait to hear what the Great Nuntius had to say.'

Together the two women set off towards the open ground near the cliff tops, where the best ground nut crops were to be found. Side by side, they looked much alike, both tall and graceful with long, raven-black hair. Although time and the harshness of their life had taken its toll on Bethan, her once slender body was now gaunt and slightly stooped, and deep lines were etched into her strong face. But her huge, blue eyes still shone with a fiery enthusiasm. She smiled, as she remembered how Adil used to say that they were 'like deep pools that a man could drown in'. Eira, buoyed up by her youthful strength, looked just like her mother, except for one startling difference. Her eyes were a deep, emerald green.

Eira worked slowly that morning as she could not get her experiences on the cliff path the previous day out of her mind. She could not wait to see her father again, and tell him what had happened. As she bent to dig for ground nuts, she inched her way inland until she could see the path her father had taken three days ago, when he set out on his journey to visit the Nuntius. This was the third day, the day that her father had said that he would return, but, she told herself, travelling was an uncertain business and he might be delayed.

She must not hope too much that he would come back today. Then, just as she was about to go back down the cliff to join the other villagers for the midday meal, she saw a figure in the distance, striding along the path. She narrowed her eyes, willing herself to see through the wisps of mist that kept drifting between her and the approaching walker. But in her heart she knew that it was her father.

For a brief moment the mist cleared, and at last she could see clearly the familiar face of the approaching figure. Her heart leapt with joy, and she ran towards him, flinging her arms around his neck. 'Father, I am so glad to see you home safely, but you look tired.'

Adil hugged his daughter and kissed her forehead. 'Eira my dear, I am glad to be home. It has been a difficult and dangerous journey, and I have much to tell you. But all in good time. Where is your mother?'

'At the bottom of the cliff I think, with the others. I came up here to watch for you. I just knew you would come back today, just as you promised.'

Adil smiled, although he felt heavy with the burden of responsibility that now rested on his shoulders. But today he would rest and enjoy the company of his family, and then tomorrow he would sit down with Eira and begin the task that had been entrusted to him.

Bethan was sitting with the other villagers. They were swapping stories and singing songs, as they rested after their morning's work. When she saw Adil approaching with Eira, her face brightened, and she jumped to her feet. Then remembering that she had an audience, she smiled and greeted her husband respectfully. He was the village Knower after all, and a certain amount of decorum had to be observed. There would be plenty of time to greet him properly when they were alone. She excused herself, and she and Adil returned to the cave that was their home. She was eager to hear about his journey and what the Great Nuntius had said.

When Bethan reached the cave, Eira had already coaxed the fire into new life and was grinding some ground nuts into a paste ready to make porridge. Adil sat by the fire, his head already nodding wearily. He was exhausted and could think only of food and sleep. She could see that she would have to wait until the following day to hear about her husband's adventures. Eira, although overjoyed to see her father again and eager to hear his news, had no idea what lay ahead. And so, she sat calmly by the fire, stirring the porridge and watching her father's eyes slowly closing, as the trials of his journey gradually slipped away.

* * *

Rain lashed the rocks outside Adil's cave. It poured in torrents past the entrance and trickled under the wooden panel that served as a door. He could not remember a storm like it. Usually the rain fell in the winter, and occasionally in the autumn, but the summers were dry and dusty. Bethan had already heard the rain beating against the door and had hurried to gather as many buckets and pans as she could find to collect the water in. Fresh water was precious and harder to find in the summer. Wind whipped the sea into huge grey waves, which crashed and roared against the cliffs. For an instant the whole cave was lit by an eerie blue light, as lightning forked across the cloud-laden sky, and thunder roared and groaned outside. The three of them sat around the fire in silence, listening to the sound of the rain. Surely it would stop soon, Eira thought to herself. Then, as if in answer to her thoughts, the sound changed from a steady roaring to an ear-splitting clatter. Eira jumped in alarm. What was that? Adil rose and, walking to the door, opened it a crack. Outside, small lumps of ice bounced off the ground, like miniature missiles. One caught Adil a stinging blow on the cheek, causing him to retreat hastily inside and shut the door with a bang. Hail in summer, he thought, his mind turning to the words of the Prophecy. Not yet snow, but perhaps this was a sign, he mused.

As the day wore on, the storm showed no signs of abating, so there was no prospect of going out foraging. They must remain confined to the cave. This, thought Adil, was the perfect opportunity for him to begin instructing Eira. But Bethan was eager to hear about his journey, and perhaps, he thought, this was a good place to begin. Huddled by the fire, the two women listened wide-eyed, as he told of his encounter with the night stalker, and gasped in relief and amazement as he explained how it had let him go unharmed.

'So compassion is not just a human characteristic is it, Father?' Eira asked.

'It would seem so, my dear. I had thought these creatures were only capable of the most hideous and savage behaviour, but I was wrong. We should not think ill of a thing simply because we do not know or understand it. All creatures are worthy of our respect, unless they prove to us that they do not deserve it.'

For some time the little family remained silent, listening to the sounds of the angry storm outside. Adil's words still hung in the air, sharp and clear like crystals, Eira thought. Her curiosity satisfied, Bethan was happy and relieved to have her husband home again. Although she knew that his journey had been of the utmost importance for them all, she had secretly hoped that it would not prove necessary. It was dangerous to cross the Great Plain, and the night stalkers were always watching for a lone, vulnerable traveller. But all was well now. He was safely back and with a message that would change everything. Dreamily she glanced around their little home. The cave was quite small, just large enough for three sleeping places and a cooking fire in the centre. The ceiling of over-hanging rock sloped sharply down towards the back of the cave until it met the floor, which was made of hard-packed mud and stones. They had been lucky enough to find a large piece of wood, which they used to block the entrance to the cave. Adil said that it must have come from the Before Peoples' time, as there were very few trees that he knew of in all the Lived-in-Lands. It kept the weather out, and so helped to keep them warm in winter. Many of their neighbours were not so fortunate, as their shelters were open to the elements, and their winters were miserably cold.

After a while Eira spoke, hesitantly at first, as she was unsure how her father would view her accident on the cliff path. He would be angry at her carelessness, she felt sure.

'Father,' she began hesitantly, 'something happened whilst you were away.' She glanced at him shyly, and he smiled encouragingly at her to continue. 'I was out foraging on the cliff tops. It was getting late, so I hurried to return home, but in the half light I missed my footing on the path and fell, knocking myself unconscious, and when I awoke, I was in the forest again.'

The indulgent smile had left her father's face and he was looking at her intently. 'Go on,' he said almost sternly.

When Eira had finished telling the story of her encounter with the stranger in the forest, Adil remained silent for a long time. The fire flickered in the darkness of the cave, casting a shadow across her father's face, concealing his expression. *What is he thinking?* she wondered. *Does he think that I am making all this up? That I'm letting my imagination run wild?* She began to fidget nervously, fearing her father's reaction. But at last he spoke.

'Eira,' he said thoughtfully, 'you are probably wondering why I made the journey to see the Nuntius, but your mother and I decided not to tell you anything until I returned. I went to consult Darius about your dreams and discuss the Prophecy with him, and he is of the same opinion as me. We think that you—and there is no easy way to say this, Eira—that you are the Chosen One.'

Bethan gasped and flung a protective arm around her daughter. 'So it's true then. But how could it be our child, Adil?'

'That is a question that only the Great Guardian can answer, but Eira's dreams speak for themselves, and the Prophecy is very clear.' Adil stared into the fire intently for a moment, before beginning to chant in a low voice:

When green-leafed tree and snow-clad hill stand together,
She will awaken and know Herself.
Then shall the Two who wander alone be joined and
*   become One.*
The Circle will complete itself and all will be made whole
*   again.*
Spring will return to the Lived-in-Lands.

'I think that it is your destiny to meet the stranger, and that you will give him a name, and when the two of you are united the world will change for all time.'

Eira gasped, her head filled with questions. 'How can this be? Am I to live in the forest forever, and what of you and Mother? Will there be a place for you there too, and what of the rest of our people? How could I leave you all here, and live happily surrounded by such beauty, knowing that you were all still struggling to live in this dark place?'

'If things are to be as I believe they are, then you need have no fears for the rest of us. All will be well, and we shall all be part of the new beginning.'

'But why me, Father?' Eira asked. She felt bewildered. After all she was just an ordinary girl. How could she hope to change the world forever?

Adil's expression softened, as he took his daughter's hand. 'None of us know the reason that we are chosen for a particular task. Only the Great Knower, whose vision spans all horizons and is beyond anything we could possibly imagine, can understand such things.'

Feeling around his neck, Adil untied the string that held the amulet Darius had given him. 'Eira my dear, I want you to have this. It was a gift from the Great Nuntius, and I believe it served me well on my journey home, protecting me from many dangers. The ancient texts say that it causes all beings that come into contact with it to be the very best that they can be,' and he held out the strange metal creature with the glittering eyes to his daughter. 'Wear it with honour and in the hope of a new beginning for us all.' With that he tied it around Eira's neck. As soon as it was in place, the eyes of the creature began to glow, flashing green.

'It's alive!' exclaimed Bethan, drawing back in alarm.

'No,' said Adil quietly, 'it has found its rightful place. Eira is its rightful mistress. She alone can truly command its power. Darius did more than he could ever know when he gave me this gift.' Then thoughtfully, he added, 'She and one other.'

Eira fingered the strange metal talisman that hung around her neck, feeling its strange warmth. It pulsed with an energy, like a living thing, and the more she looked at it the more she was sure that it was moving, but not here, somewhere else. But that was absurd; it didn't make sense. It was just a beautiful piece of jewellery, like the Before People used to wear. And she was just about to ask her father what he meant, when there was a loud banging at the door. Through the din of the hail, they could hear voices outside, shouting.

'Respected Knower, Adil, please may we come in? We have been driven from our homes by the storm, and we seek shelter,' several voices called out urgently. Jumping to his feet, Adil rushed to open the door. Standing outside were a small group of villagers, all soaked to the skin and trembling with cold.

'Come in, dear friends, warm yourselves by the fire,' he said. 'Bethan, do we have any food? Can we feed our poor neighbours?'

'There is a little broth left,' Bethan replied, her hand already reaching for the ladle. Carefully she measured out what remained of the steaming gruel and handed it to the shivering group.

As night fell, they huddled together in the little cave, listening to the sounds of the storm which continued to rage outside, and which showed no sign of abating. As they sat crowded together, a small voice piped up, 'Mr Knower, will you tell us a story? I'm frightened.' Searching amongst the group to see where the voice had come from, Adil smiled broadly as his gaze fell on a small, tousled head. Sandwiched tightly between her parents, sat a little girl no more than five years old. A rare sight in the village these days, he thought with a pang of sadness. As long as he could remember, only a handful of children had been born to the villagers.

'And what sort of story would you like to hear, young lady?' he asked, his eyes twinkling with amusement.

'The people before, the people before, and monsters,' came the excited reply.

'Ah, the Before People,' Adil mused, pretending to think deeply. 'What can I tell you of them I wonder.'

'Tell us what the world was like in those days', another voice piped up.

'And about the animals that lived with them,' added

the little girl's mother, looking down indulgently at her young daughter.

'Well,' said Adil, scanning the expectant faces in front of him and pausing for effect, like the experienced storyteller that he was. 'Long, long ago, before any of you were even thought of, there lived a people,' he began. 'They lived right here where we live now, but there were trees and grass, and the sun shone bright and yellow like a great big ball, warming the ground and the things that lived and grew there. There were lots of children', and he smiled at the little girl, 'and the sea was a deep azure blue, filled with fishes and strange creatures that lived half in the sea and half on the land. The Before People had legends, which said that these strange creatures were half man, half fish, but these were just stories, perhaps from a time before even the Before People came to live by the sea—who knows?' And the small group sighed in wonder and amazement, despite the fact that most of them had heard these same stories many times before. But Adil had a knack of recounting the legends in such a way that it seemed to the listener that he was hearing them for the first time, no matter how well he knew the story.

'The people lived here for a long time, enjoying the beauty and bounty of the land, but gradually they became greedy and wanted more than the land could give them, so they began to fight amongst themselves and steal from one another. Then, as matters got worse, and there were shortages of things for some caused by the greed of others, they began to kill one another. A thing previously unheard of. Slowly they divided themselves up into different groups and travelled around this globe, dividing it up into what they called countries. These countries guarded their resources, food, water, fuel, and precious metals dug from beneath the ground, fiercely fighting each other to keep their share of the land, and they called these large fights between countries "wars".

'Slowly, as more and more people were born, they had to devise ways of feeding all the hungry mouths, and so they invented machines to do some of the work for them. And when they could no longer rely on gathering what grew naturally around them, they had to force the earth to produce more and more food. They dug holes in the rocks and extracted metals, which they fashioned into objects, tools to do their work for them, and also objects of beauty to adorn themselves with. These were often made of a yellow metal they called gold. It was soft and beautiful and shone like the sun. Many wars were fought and many people killed in pursuit of this yellow metal.

'But after a while even this wasn't enough, and they wanted more. They squandered the globe's resources, and so the metals that they dug from the earth and even the water they drank became scarce. The people began to starve and to die. At this time, there were in the world clever men and women who had mastered to some degree the laws that govern how living things and the earth itself work. These men and women decided to breed a race of creatures to do the work that people had done. A long time before this the people had forced others of their kind to work for them for nothing, and they had called this "slavery". In time, they came to realise the cruelty and injustice of enslaving others of their own kind, but now there was a way of using slaves without being troubled about their welfare. They felt no guilt when they looked beneath the veil that concealed the secrets of existence. When they saw the beauty of the pattern that dictated how each creature should look and behave, they said in their arrogance: "We can improve on this. We can make something more suited to the modern world and to our needs."'

As he continued with his tale, Adil remembered his encounter with the night stalker in the tunnel and the words that it had spoken to him, and he felt a sudden pang of pity. These creatures had not asked to be made, but they had to live with the folly of their creators, who themselves were now long dead. But perhaps, he thought, the Great Wisdom had some other destiny for them, as yet unknown to mortal beings.

His audience waited patiently for him to continue the story, but when he did not, they nodded silently to each other in agreement, and began to make themselves as comfortable as they could to pass the rest of the night. The Respected Knower must be tired. After all, he had only just returned from a long and difficult journey. They should let him rest, and besides, they knew that he would be happy to continue with his tale whenever they asked him. Soon the little band were all asleep. Only Adil remained awake, staring into the embers of the fire. He could not get the memory of his encounter with the night stalker out of his mind.

As dawn broke the wind dropped almost as suddenly as it had begun to blow, and slowly the drumming of the rain quietened. Gingerly, Adil pushed open the door and peered outside. He let out a gasp of amazement at the sight that met his eyes. The ever-present, grey mist was gone, and the sky was lit by the golden rays of the sun which had pierced the leaden clouds. But the thing that caused him to stand transfixed with awe, was the sight of a rainbow, something he had never seen before. He had read about these beautiful sky arches, as he called them, in the writings of the Before People, but to see such a sight was a gift beyond his wildest dreams. Tears of joy streaming down his face, he called to the others to come and look.

Rushing out of the cave in answer to his urgent cries, the little band stood, frozen, taking in the scene before them, their faces filled with awe and wonder. They whispered quietly to each other, almost as if the sound of their voices would cause this beautiful vision to disappear. 'Respected Knower,' one of the group asked, 'what does this mean? Is it a sign for us?'

Adil, who was as awestruck as the rest of them, replied in measured tones. 'This, my friends, is a great wonder, and I shall have to reflect on its significance. But of one thing I am sure: it is a sign of hope. Never before in the memory of our people has such a thing been seen. Never before has the sun shone through the clouds, and the wind chased away the grey mists. More than that I cannot say, at least for the moment.' With that he was silent, and no amount of persuasion would induce him to say more. He held up his hand, as if to ward off their questions, and eventually retreated back into the cave, shutting the door firmly behind him.

Eira, who had remained outside with the villagers,

continued to stand looking up at the rainbow, drinking in the warmth of the sun's rays. It was so beautiful. So many colours! She struggled to remember the names of them all, as she had seen it written in the ancient books. Red, orange, yellow, green, blue, indigo, and what was the last one? Something like a flower— yes, that was it: violet! But why was it there? Was it connected with the storm? But they had had bad storms before, and nothing like this had ever happened. It was almost as if that other world, which she had visited in her dreams, was trying to find its way here into this world. But that could not be, could it? Unconsciously her hand strayed to the strange amulet around her neck. Feeling it beneath her fingers, she started. She could have sworn that it had moved when she touched it. It felt warm and soft like a living thing. She pulled her hand away in panic, but when she looked down at it, the amulet appeared just as it had before. A small, curiously shaped metal creature with glowing, green eyes, cold and inanimate.

Some of the villagers were staring at her, and Eira began to feel uncomfortable. Perhaps they had seen the amulet and wondered what it was. Slowly, and, she hoped, casually, she walked away from the little crowd, and on up the cliff path, putting as much distance between herself and the whispering villagers as she could. When she reached the cliff top she sat down on a small flat rock, her favourite spot for looking out to sea, and turned to gaze once more at the rainbow. To her disappointment it was fading rapidly, and the rays of the sun were once again almost obscured by the familiar thick, grey cloud. Looking down, she saw little wisps of mist winding themselves around her ankles. So this was just a taste, a tantalising hint of the beauty she had witnessed in that other world. The briefest of glimpses, like the scent of blossom caught on the wind. But she would always remember it, she thought to herself fiercely; no one could take that from her now.

There in the gathering gloom she remained for some time, her mind drifting and her heart filled with longing for the forest and the mysterious, elusive stranger. The sight of the rainbow had seemed to strengthen her connection and her longing for that other place. Perhaps the two worlds were drifting closer together, like two ships on the ocean, she thought, caught on the tide, pulled by the currents. Perhaps there were currents in time and space too. Great ocean waves and little tidal pools, where a world could get caught up on the rocks and then be pulled clear by a sudden surge. Perhaps the storm they had just experienced was such a tidal surge, which had caused the two worlds to touch for a short time. Then she shrugged; goodness knows what had made her think such a thing, and with a shiver she rose to her feet. It was getting cold; she should return home. She had a strong feeling that her father wanted to talk to her urgently.

Chapter 6

The cave door was still firmly shut when she got home, and Eira had to use all her weight to open it. Inside, she found her father sitting alone, his head bowed, shoulders hunched. At first she thought he was asleep, but then she heard him sigh. Hearing the sound of the door opening, he looked up, and there was a troubled expression on his face. Seeing her, he smiled, and holding out his arm said, 'Eira my dear, come and sit with me; we have much to discuss.'

Slipping quickly to his side, Eira dropped down gently onto the ground next to her father and took his hand. 'Father, what is it? Something is troubling you; please tell me. The world is changing, isn't it? You say that I will be a part of this change, but I don't understand how, or how I can return to the forest and meet the stranger there. After all, I only dreamt of that place. It cannot be real can it?'

For a while Adil was silent, then, as if choosing his words with great care, he said, 'Eira, the world of dreams is not always what it appears to be. Sometimes, it is a way of showing us another reality, something that exists just as truly as this place here and now. And sometimes it is not another place that a dream shows us but another way of thinking or viewing the world that we already inhabit. A dream is like a window and rarely, as I believe is the case with your dreams, a doorway into another reality. Somehow you were able to step through the doorway and inhabit that other world for a while. I do not understand how this was possible, but I believe that such things do not happen by chance. There is always a reason when such great events occur. It is up to us to follow the thread, to believe in the ultimate goodness that exists within all things, and to allow ourselves to be guided by that.'

Eira thought for a moment, then she asked, 'And what of the amulet, Father? Where did it come from? Is it magic?'

Adil laughed. 'What is magic?'

'I, I don't know,' Eira replied thoughtfully. 'I suppose it is something completely out of the ordinary, something that we cannot find an explanation for.'

'Indeed it is that,' Adil replied cautiously, 'but it is also much more than that. It is an understanding and an unshakeable belief in what is, the fundamental "realness" of a thing. When you know what something really is, what it is meant to be, then you can command it, and that is what we call magic. But the use of such knowledge is forbidden,' he added darkly.

'And the amulet?' she asked again.

'The amulet is a link with a different reality. It is the physical representative in this world of something that cannot be present here—indeed the Great Guardian would not allow it. Something whose presence would be far too powerful for us to endure. It is what we call a symbol.'

Both remained deep in thought for a time, the silence broken only by the sound of a small creature scratching in the mud at the back of the cave. Eventually Eira said quietly, 'So when I felt the amulet move, that was the real creature that the amulet represents, moving around in its own world.'

Adil turned and, regarding his daughter narrowly, asked, 'When did this happen?'

'Just after we saw the rainbow and the sun shining through the clouds. It felt alive, all smooth and warm, like a living thing, but when I looked at it, it was just a piece of metal. The villagers were staring at me, so I walked up the cliff to get away from them,' she added.

Hesitantly, Adil replied, 'I am not certain why the creature moves in this world, but I believe it has something to do with the bridge between our world and the one you visited in your dreams. Somehow, the creature that the amulet symbolises bridges the two worlds and makes a connection between them possible.'

Sitting cross legged beside her father, Eira cupped her hand over the strange object hanging around her neck and felt it pulsing, like a heartbeat, she thought. And as she did so, she became aware of the same fragrance that had filled the air in her dream. Closing her eyes, she tried to imagine herself back there, sitting on the warm grass, listening to the sound of birds in the trees, drifting, drifting.

* * *

Striding up the side of a small hill, he caught the scent of an unfamiliar smell in the air. It was like nothing he had ever experienced before: sharp, fresh, and there was a burning sensation that went with it, a bit like the heat of the sun, but somehow different. But he had no words for this new sensation. Looking down at his arm he saw strange little lumps appearing between the hairs, then an odd shiver overcame him. What could it be? He shook himself to ward off this uncomfortable feeling and continued on up the hill. From the top he could see a great distance out across the tops of the trees, but this time, to his amazement, a very different sight met his eyes. Instead of the green canopy of the forest stretching far into the distance, there was a white mist which covered everything, obscuring the trees from view, and it seemed to be filled with tiny little flakes. Some of the flakes settled on his arm, only to disappear before he could study them more closely. What could this mean?

As he watched, the uncomfortable sensation increased, and so did the white flakes. They continued to fall from the sky at such a rate and so thickly that he could no longer see the forest at all. There were now so many of them that they covered the ground, and his feet sank into them as he walked, making a crunching sound. As he lifted his foot, he could see that it left a mark where he had trodden on the white flakes.

Feeling bewildered and shivering with cold, although he was not able to put a name to the sensation, he turned and ran down the hill, slipping and sliding in the all-enveloping, white blanket as he went. Once back in the wood, he sheltered under the spreading branches of a great tree, and watched the curious, tiny white leaves fall. Could this be the autumn that the Wisdom had spoken of? But no, it could not be, as the green leaves were still on the trees, and the Wisdom had said that they would turn brown and fall to the ground when autumn came. But then what were the tiny white leaves?

For what seemed like a very long time he crouched and shivered under the great tree, but then, like the sun breaking through the clouds after a shower of rain, a thought came into his head. This would soon pass, and the sun would shine again and take away the unpleasant sensation of cold. Yes, that is what this strange sensation was: it was cold, and as he watched, the tiny white leaves ceased to fall and began to disappear from the ground before his astonished eyes. The sun appeared as if from nowhere, pushing back the last remnants of grey cloud. Warmth returned, and once again he became aware of the sound of birdsong. Until that moment he hadn't realised that the falling white leaves had brought with them a muffled silence. All the creatures of the forest had fallen silent, but now he noticed that they had begun to call to one another and move about the forest again.

His mind turned to thoughts of the other creature that looked so like him. How had it faired during this strange time? Had it been puzzled or afraid? He wanted to find it and think his thoughts out loud to it. Lead it to the warmth of the sun. Reassure it that the Wisdom had told him that the cold would pass. Anxiously, he paced through the forest, restlessly searching for it, but it was nowhere to be found. Once he thought that he caught a glimpse of its slight figure reflected in a forest pool, but when he raced to the other side, to his disappointment he found that it was only the shadow of a weeping willow tree, bending over the water.

A great wave of emptiness engulfed him, and he lifted his head and shouted his thoughts to the forest. 'Where are you, reflection of me? Please let me see you again! I want to speak my thoughts to you. To see you reflected in my eyes.' But all that he heard was the gentle calls of his animal companions and the breath of the wind in the trees.

* * *

Bethan returned with a basket full of ground nuts, and some small green plants which she had picked at the base of the cliffs. Walking into the cave, she found her husband and daughter sitting in silence, both as still as statues, eyes staring at the ground. Neither of them looked up as she entered. In fact, it was some time and much clanking and banging of pots before they became aware of her presence.

'Oh, Eira,' Bethan exclaimed in annoyance, 'you've let the fire go out!'

'Don't scold her, my dear,' Adil said gently. 'It's my fault for keeping her talking, but we had important matters to discuss, and so I am afraid all other considerations were forgotten for a time. Here, let me help you. I will go and fetch some twigs to get it going again. Eira, help your mother now, will you.'

Eira stood up and, as if in a dream, began to sort and clean the ground nuts ready to make a broth. Her mother kept giving her sharp, penetrating looks, but Eira, who was oblivious to her mother's scrutiny, seemed to drift back and forth between the sunlit landscape of the other world and the more familiar, grey, forbidding scene of her home. For a moment, she felt sure that she saw snow falling in the forest, but it must be her imagination, surely. It was summer there, as it was here too. But wait—was that a voice calling her? A man's voice calling in despair, 'Where are you?' It drifted on the forest air like an echo and then faded sadly away.

She became aware that her parents were looking at her intently, and her father said, 'Are you all right, Eira? Is something troubling you?'

'It's nothing but a daydream I'm sure, but I thought I saw snow in the forest and heard a voice calling out to me, a man's voice; he was looking for me, desperately searching,' she replied, perplexed.

Adil frowned and again his mind turned to the words of the Prophecy: *When green-leafed tree and snow-clad hill stand together....* But it had been a daydream, nothing more, probably brought on by their conversation and the storm the previous day, he thought to himself.

He patted his daughter's arm reassuringly. No need to trouble her further at present; she had had to absorb enough today as it was. For the moment he would say nothing. 'Yes, yes, my dear, I'm sure you're right; just a daydream.' He smiled, and returned to the task of rekindling the fire.

* * *

The next morning Adil rose early, as he planned to visit some of the numerous caves that peppered the cliffs along the coast line just below the village. Some were accessible from above via steep paths which tested the nimblest of climbers, but the most interesting and mysterious caves could only be reached from the sea.

Adil's people had never spent much time at sea. There were no fish, or at least so they thought, and the knowledge of what lay across the sea had been lost a long time ago. Besides, it was no easy task, as the materials to build a boat were scarce. However, Adil had, by dint of patient perseverance over the course of many years, managed to collect enough drift wood to construct a small rowing boat. He kept it hidden in one of the few dry caves down on a little stretch of beach just below his home. It was to this small patch of beach that he made his way that morning. He set off whilst the rest of the community were still asleep, as he did not want anyone to see him leave and start asking awkward questions. He preferred that the caves and what they contained should remain a secret, at least for the moment.

He planned to take Eira to the caves and show her what he had discovered, but not today. Today he wanted to be alone, as he had much to think about, and the caves were a very good place for thinking. Gingerly, he picked his way down the cliff path, feeling his way carefully in the half light of dawn. This morning there was no sign of the shining, yellow sun that had greeted them the previous day. The sky had returned to its usual leaden grey, and only a thin, yellow streak of sunlight illuminated the dawn sky. But the sight of the sun yesterday had given him hope. It was a sign; he could feel it in the air. A sign that something immensely powerful was stirring, and that it was about to change their world for ever.

Finally, he felt the crunch of shingle beneath his feet and breathed a sigh of relief. He had never had much of a head for heights, and he did not enjoy the climb down the cliffs, but it was worth it, he told himself. His feet sank deeply into the piles of tiny stones which covered the little cove as he trudged slowly towards a small opening at the base of the cliff face. Inside was a boat barely large enough for two people. It was made from an assortment of bits and pieces, mainly oddly shaped scraps of wood. There were, however, other, unknown materials incorporated into its hull. Sheets of a strange, smooth, flexible material formed the curving prow and the underside of the tiny vessel. Adil had no idea what they were, or where they came from, but they served the purpose very well. Lying inside the makeshift craft were two short poles, each with a small piece of metal with odd markings on it, tied firmly to the end. These served as oars.

Grasping the prow with both hands, he dragged the boat down to the shore. It was hard work, as the stones were so deep that both he and his craft sank into them by several inches with every step, but at last he reached the sea. Breathing heavily, he straightened, and, wiping his brow, stood gazing out across the ocean. He wondered what lay beyond the horizon. Maybe there was another land, but what was it like? Perhaps it had not been ruined long ago, as this place had been, and it stood green and fertile, its trees heavy with fruit, just waiting to be discovered. He sighed, for he knew that this could not be. The Wisdom, which the Knowers passed down from generation to generation, was very clear on the matter. The whole globe was sleeping under a grey mist, and their only hope was the Prophecy.

He climbed into the dinghy, and as he did so, his gaze fell on the stones at his feet. Amongst them something small and white shone, catching the reflected light off the water. He bent down and sinking his fingers into the surrounding gravel, pulled out a tiny, conical-shaped object. Cradling it in the palm of his hand, he stood transfixed, marvelling at the exquisite workmanship of this miniature work of art. *Who could have made such a thing?* he wondered. No bigger than the nail on his little finger, it was translucent white, made from a kind of material that he had never seen before. It looked a little like bone but much thinner, and was formed into a series of spirals, each one smaller than the last, until at its point the spirals were so tiny as to be almost too small for him to see, but the pattern remained faithful to the end. What could it be? Carefully he placed the tiny object in his bag. He would study it later and show it to Eira. It would delight her, he was sure. Thought-fully, he pushed the wooden craft into the surf, jumped in, and pushed off into the ebbing tide.

Cautiously at first, Adil manoeuvred the boat out

into the current which flowed around the base of the cliffs. It was a tricky business, and he was not a practised oarsman, but eventually he managed to set a course for a line of dark openings in the base of the cliff, about two miles along the coast from his little bay. These caves were his destination, and he hoped to be able to sail into the largest of them. If his memory served him correctly, there was a small outcrop of rocks just inside the opening where he could moor his craft. From there he should be able to find a way into the cave system.

As he had hoped, the current took him and brought him close into the cliffs at just the right point. As he steered into the cave mouth, he was hit by an enormous swell that threatened to capsize the boat. Struggling frantically against the powerful, backward flow of the wave, he eventually managed to guide his craft into calmer waters. Shaking with exhaustion and fright, he drew up against the natural jetty inside the rocky haven. Quickly he secured the boat, and with a sigh of relief, stepped out onto dry land.

Now he was at leisure to explore his surroundings. Although he had been here several times before, this place never ceased to fill him with a sense of wonder. The rocky walls soared high above his head, so that he could hardly make out the roof of the cave in the moisture-laden air. The sound of waves breaking on the rocks outside echoed around the enclosed space with a deafening roar. Picking his way over the slippery rocks, he headed for the back of the cavern.

He ran his hand along the wall, searching for a small opening that led into a series of passageways.

These rocky corridors fed into other, connecting caves further inland. The caves there were always dry, as the ground sloped gently upwards, keeping them safe from flooding. Deep underground they had remained untouched by the ruinous activities of the Before People. Perhaps the sea level had dropped since those terrible times, opening the way into this undiscovered world.

He edged his way slowly along the back wall of the cavern, and eventually his hand reached into an open space. *Ah, this must be it,* he thought, as further exploration revealed a hole large enough for him to squeeze through. Cautiously, he wriggled through the narrow opening. Here it was pitch black, but he knew from previous experience that the inner caves were lit by a mysterious light, and soon he would be able to see his way without difficulty. Progress was slow, however, and the floor of the passageway uneven, but after a while he saw a ghostly glow in the distance, which told him that he had almost reached his destination.

Adil gasped, as he stepped out into this secret, rocky hideaway deep beneath the earth and looked around him. The source of the ghostly light was plain. The walls of the cavern were covered in a kind of crystal which sparkled and shone, transforming the gloom into an enchanted grotto. He could hear the trickle of water somewhere, and looking to his left he saw huge columns of smooth, white rocks towering above his head, glistening with moisture. From the ceiling, similar columns hung down, impossibly suspended as if in mid air, dripping water from their tips onto the rising columns below.

Navigating a course between the glistening columns, he made his way to the side wall of the cavern, peering intently at the shadow-covered walls as he went. At last, there it was, the thing he had been searching for. He had felt sure it was in this cave, although it was more than a year since he had been here. But he could hardly forget how he had felt when he first entered the cave and saw the white columns of rock shining in the unearthly light shed by the crystal walls. Then as if that were not wonder enough, he had seen it. Right there, on the side wall behind the columns. He could hardly believe his eyes. At first he had thought it was a trick of the light, but when he looked more closely he saw that it was real and not just a figment of his imagination.

He scrambled over a pile of loose rocks just below the wall, and there it was: a life-size drawing of a man. Beside the man was a strange creature, which he could not identify, even though he had seen many pictures of animals in the Before Peoples' books. It had a delicate, graceful body and long, curling horns. Its head was lowered, as if it were paying homage to the man, who stood looking out across the cave, his eyes staring into the distance as though he were searching for something.

Adil stood gazing, spellbound, at the images for a long time. Who could have drawn them and when? The man was naked, and he knew that the Before People had worn clothes. Did this mean that the pictures had been drawn by a more ancient people? The outlines had been fashioned using a black substance, and the rest filled in with beautiful, vibrant colours which looked as fresh now as the day they were painted.

Somehow he knew that these images were important, that they were connected with what was happening now, and that he must show them to Eira. He had a sudden conviction that she alone could shed light on their origin and their present significance. Finally, tearing himself away from the regal figure and his animal companion, who seemed to be watching over their surroundings, he turned to go. As he clambered back over the rocks towards the tunnel entrance, he had a sudden urge to explore further. There was a side tunnel off to his left just large enough for him to walk down without having to stoop. He had a little time before the tide changed. Perhaps there were more paintings further on, he thought.

The passageway was longer than he had anticipated, and it took him quite a while to reach the next cave. By the time he got there he was tired and hungry. He had brought a little food with him, and so when the way finally opened out into another cavern even larger than the first, he made himself comfortable on a small rock where he tucked hungrily into his meal. As he ate, he began to study his surroundings. He had never been in this cave before, and looking around he could see that it was vast. The vaulted roof soared high above his head, and he could barely make out the walls in the dim light, as although they were encrusted with the same glowing crystal as the previous cave, it did not appear to give out as much light.

When he had finished eating, he decided to explore the cavern before returning to the boat. It would be a pity to have come so far and not see whatever wonders he was sure lay hidden here too. Feeling his way carefully in the half light, he decided to try and find the walls of the cave so that he could judge its true size. The floor was covered in tiny, needle-sharp crystals which hurt his feet. Perhaps they are the children of those mighty columns he had seen in the last cavern, he mused. After several minutes of careful progress, his hand finally touched the rocky boundary which marked the extent of the great vault.

Peering deeper into the shadows, he realised that there was something painted on the wall. As he approached, he could just make out in the dim light the form of a young woman. She too was naked, like the painting of the man in the other cave, and like him she gazed out of the picture as if searching for something. That there should be a picture of a woman as well as a man did not strike Adil as particularly odd, but what made him gasp with astonishment, and sent him reeling backwards onto the sharp, crystal bed, was the sight of what the woman was holding. Cradled in the palm of her left hand was the exact likeness of the amulet he had given Eira. It had been painted in the most vibrant yellow, and the eyes of the strange creature glowed a piercing green. On closer examination, he realised that the eyes were not painted at all, but where inset, precious stones, which sparkled and shone with an eerie light.

Adil slumped to the ground, his whole body trembling with excitement. What could this mean? Was the amulet which Eira wore as ancient as this painting? Had it been fashioned by the same people who had drawn these images? Questions flooded his mind, but time was short. The tide would soon be changing, and if he did not leave soon he would be trapped here until the next tide. Rubbing his sore feet, he got up stiffly and was just about to leave the cavern to begin his journey back to the boat, when something else caught his eye. Almost obscured by a huge pillar of crystal, was yet another painting. Scarcely able to contain himself, Adil scrambled around the rocky formation and there, smiling down at him, was a picture of the man and the woman standing together. Their hands were entwined, and they were surrounded by an assortment of animals, some of which he knew, and others, which were completely unknown to him. Around their necks they wore identical amulets, both of which had green eyes fashioned from the same precious stones.

This final revelation was too much for poor Adil who, blinded by tears, began his painstaking journey back to the shore. This was the Prophecy, of that he was sure. Put here in the far distant past by a people wiser than those who came after them, in the hope that someone would find their message and understand it. Hidden below the ground, for how long he could not say. How many races and peoples had come and gone whilst these images smiled down from the crystal-covered walls, waiting to impart their message when the time was right.

Now he must go home. Now more than ever, he must try and help Eira understand the importance of her dreams and visions. He would bring her here and show her the paintings. Then she would not doubt herself anymore. Perhaps, he thought, if she saw the pictures, it would help her to strengthen her link with the world of her dreams, and then one day she would stand hand-in-hand with the stranger from the forest. But he would no longer be a stranger, and he would bear the name that she would give him. They would all feel the warmth of the sun again and see in reality some of the creatures who stood with the couple in the painting. All would be healed. All would be made new again. He bit his bottom lip, as his heart swelled with an almost unbearable feeling of joy.

Hastening through the narrow passageways back to the little landing place, he couldn't get the picture of the woman's face out of his mind. Perhaps it was his imagination, but to him she looked so like his beloved daughter that it was uncanny. But of course, that was impossible. The woman in the painting, if she had ever lived at all, had lived such a long time ago that it was almost beyond reckoning. But the feeling remained with him all the way home.

Piloting the makeshift craft back to his own little stretch of beach was no easy task, as now the current was against him. It took him several attempts before he was able to clear the shore and head for the open sea, as each time he pushed off into the current it swept him back onto the beach. But at last he reached the deep water and began paddling frantically. It was getting late, and it would be almost dark by the time he reached the cove. Suppressing a sudden wave of panic, he tried to concentrate on paddling. He had lingered far too long in the caves. How could he have been so foolish! At that moment, something large and shiny slid silently past the boat. It came so close that it almost collided with it, and its wake caused his fragile craft to bob and lurch alarmingly.

Once again panic threatened to overwhelm him. What could it be? It was said that there were no creatures in the sea anywhere in the Lived-in-Lands. But this, although he had only caught a glimpse of it, was most certainly a living thing. He decided that now was not the time to seek the creature out. Dusk was falling, and he could only just make out the faint silhouette of the familiar outcrop of rocks which marked his landing place. He must make haste.

He risked another quick scan of the ocean, peering down into the inky blackness of the water below him in search of the mysterious sea creature, but he could see nothing. Then, taking up the oars, he made one last, desperate push for the shore. At last the boat touched solid ground, and climbing wearily out he dragged it up the beach, slipping and sliding on the greasy deposits that the tide always left as it sucked and gurgled over the stones.

Above the dull, grating sound of the boat's keel dragging through the shingle, he became aware of a low, mournful groaning. It sounded like someone or something in pain, he thought. He paused and stood still for a moment, listening, trying to work out where the sound was coming from. Then he saw it. A small black outline further up the beach, close to the little cave where he kept his boat, and it was moving. About the size of a small child, its head was not unlike the pictures he had seen of creatures the Before People had called dogs. Every now and again it would lift its head and cry plaintively. It did not seem to have any feet, just flat, paddle-shaped limbs a little like the fins of a fish, he decided.

The creature appeared to be in distress, and Adil was a kind-hearted man. He could not leave it to suffer, not without at least trying to help. Screwing up his courage, he approached the wailing animal. When it saw him it tried to retreat, but it seemed to have difficulty moving, although it did not appear to be injured, and then he saw the source of its distress. Somehow one of its front limbs had become trapped between two rocks which now held it firmly, preventing it from escaping.

He approached cautiously, thinking that the creature would almost certainly try to defend itself if it felt threatened. Talking gently and reassuringly, he approached it from the side, trying to avoid its head, and then, grabbing its front leg firmly with both hands, he pulled. The animal's skin was slippery, and he found it difficult to keep a hold, but summoning all his strength he pushed and pulled again. With a sudden cry of what he guessed to be alarm and probably pain, the creature's limb came free, and staggering backwards Adil watched it make its way down the beach with surprising speed.

Then, with a splash it was in the water and swimming. Seconds later it was out of sight. Breathing hard, Adil was about to finish stowing the boat, when from the sea there came a deafening roar. The sound froze him to the spot with terror. He had never heard such a noise before. Reluctantly, he turned and looked out to sea, terrified by the prospect of what he might see. But he was greeted by the sight of the mysterious creature that he had encountered on his return journey, and swimming by its side was the animal that he had just rescued. The giant monster must be its mother, he thought smiling, as he watched them disappear into the darkness. So there *was* life in the ocean after all.

Chapter 7

Eira was standing in the doorway, peering into the darkness, when Adil walked wearily up the path. 'He's back,' she called over her shoulder to her mother, when she caught sight of her father trudging up the narrow track from the beach. Bethan rushed to greet her husband with a look of relief on her face.

'Where have you been? We've been so worried about you,' she said, a hint of tension in her voice. 'When you didn't come back at sunset, I thought you'd drowned. I do wish you wouldn't go out in that boat Adil. It's full of holes.'

Adil smiled fondly at his wife. He could hardly blame her for worrying. It had been dark for some time now, and he had indeed been risking his life visiting the caves in his makeshift boat. Should he tell them both about his encounter with the mysterious creature? he wondered, or perhaps it would be better to wait until the morning, as he had a lot to tell. 'I'm sorry my dear,' he said tenderly. 'I didn't mean to worry you, but I found something so wonderful in the caves that I stayed a little longer than I should. But all's well now. I'm back safe and sound.'

Eira, who had been watching her father anxiously all this time, asked eagerly, 'And what did you find, Father?'

Adil turned and, regarding his daughter with a grave expression, said quietly, 'I discovered a thing so wonderful that I hardly know how to begin to tell you. But it's late, so perhaps we should wait until the morning, and we will talk of it then.' He hesitated, as he did not want to cause Bethan further worry by adding that he wanted to take Eira back to the caves with him to see the paintings. He would have to choose the right moment and break it to her gently. Yawning widely, he excused himself from further questioning and lay down by the fire to sleep.

Eira gave a little sigh of frustration. She was burning with curiosity, and questions were falling over themselves in her mind. She was desperate to know what her father had discovered in the caves, but she would have to wait until morning now. Her father was asleep and she did not dare to wake him.

* * *

The following morning all three were up bright and early. Bethan, who had stayed at home the previous day to watch for Adil, was getting ready to go foraging with the other villagers. Usually Eira went with her mother, but today she was excused, as Bethan knew that her husband needed to talk to their daughter. She too was curious about the discovery in the caves, but she was a patient woman, and besides, she knew that Adil would tell her soon enough. She could wait. All would be revealed in due course, of that she was certain.

When her mother had gone, leaving the two of them alone with strict instructions not to let the fire go out, Eira turned and gave her father a pleading look. She could wait no longer. She *must* know what he had seen in the caves the previous day. Adil had, despite appearances to the contrary, spent much of the night awake, going over his experiences in the cave and puzzling over the best way to explain it all to Eira without exposing her to the dangers of a journey to the caverns. But, he decided, it was the only way for her to understand. She must see the paintings for herself. He would take her there today.

Rising to his feet and offering Eira his hand, he said, 'I saw something in the caverns yesterday which I think concerns you and your elusive stranger. I feel that it is terribly important for you to see it for yourself. For only then will you truly understand the significance of your dreams. So,' he added firmly, 'we must take the boat out again today and visit the caves.'

Adil felt a mixture of foreboding and exhilaration at the prospect of repeating his experiences of the previous day, but he was cheered by his daughter's reaction. Eira gasped with excitement. Although, she admitted secretly to herself, she was just a little afraid, as she had never been in a boat before. In fact she had never even seen a boat, and the very thought of floating about on the surface of that huge body of forbidding grey water, its mysterious depths stretching far below, filled her with foreboding. But her father obviously thought the trip important enough to risk the perilous journey two days running, and if he was willing to go, then so was she!

Together they made their way down the cliff path to the little inlet where Adil kept his boat. 'Mother will be very angry that we have gone and left the fire to go out,' Eira said to her father.

With a slight note of impatience in his voice, Adil replied, 'Sometimes, there are more important things to be done than staying at home tending the fire! Fires can always be relit, but if the Call goes out, and you do not answer it, then no amount of fire tending will bring that lost opportunity back again. Come,' he said curtly, 'the tide is about to turn. If we hurry, it will carry us easily to the next inlet.'

Adil quickened his pace, and Eira had to run to keep up with him. Their feet sinking into the deep shingle on the beach, they soon reached the overhanging rocks which sheltered Adil's little boat, and between them they dragged it down to the water. The task was much easier with two, and soon they were riding the surf, from where they quickly pushed off into deeper water.

Eira clung to the sides of the boat. The unfamiliar lurching and bobbing motion made her feel queasy. Before them was the open sea stretching to the far horizon and, her father said, way beyond that to no one knew where. Looking down into the murky, grey opaqueness of the water, she fancied she saw a huge shape gliding past just below the boat, but no, it must have been her imagination; there were no living creatures in the sea anymore. Suddenly the boat gave a lurch and yawed violently to the right. They had been caught by the current and it was pulling them towards a large outcrop of rocks which tumbled into the sea, looking for all the world like a huge, ruined castle. Just like the pictures she had seen in the Before Peoples' books, Eira thought.

'Don't be alarmed,' her father said. 'The current is taking us to the next inlet, which is where the entrance to the caves is to be found. We can let the sea do the work for us until we are nearer to the shore, then we must paddle for all we are worth to overcome the current and propel the boat into calmer waters.' As they rounded the rocky outcrop, Adil handed Eira a short paddle. Taking the two short oars with the metal tips himself, he proceeded to guide the boat out of the current. 'Use your paddle to steer the back of the boat if it swings around into the current again,' he shouted over the roar of the surf which crashed onto the rocks above them.

At last they reached the calmer, shallower waters near the shore, and Adil began to row until they were close in under the overhanging rocks of the cliff face. He was searching for the inlet which led to the cavern where he had moored his boat yesterday. 'Ah, there it is.' A huge opening in the rocks almost sucked them in with the inflowing water. Adil rowed cautiously into the cave and manoeuvred the boat until it was resting alongside a large, flat rock, which served as a natural landing place.

Tying the boat carefully to a small splinter of rock which protruded from the otherwise smooth surface, he helped Eira out of the boat. Unsteadily she climbed out onto dry land and began to study her surroundings. Gradually, as her eyes became accustomed to the gloom, she was able to make out the vast, vaulted ceiling way above her head. The cavern was enormous, their little jetty dwarfed by the huge, slippery black rocks, which jutted out from the cave walls into the sea. 'At one time, long ago, these caves would have been home to a myriad of different creatures, and the sea itself would have been teaming with life,' her father said wistfully. 'But now there is only the sea,' he sighed.

Eira, too, felt a terrible sadness at the loss, but then her thoughts turned to her dreams of the forest warmed by the sun and full of life, and she felt her heart swelling with a new sense of hope. It would not always be like this, she thought. Something was changing. She could feel it. Then she remembered the dark shape she had half glimpsed, gliding beneath their boat. Should she tell her father, she wondered. Or had it just been an illusion, caused by the play of light, or the shadow of the rocks on the water. No, she must tell him. Perhaps he knew something about it, even if it was only a trick of the light.

Hesitantly she said, 'There is nothing living in the sea, is there, Father?'

Adil gave his daughter a searching look. Had she caught a glimpse of the creatures he had seen yesterday? he wondered. 'Why do you ask?' he replied cautiously. He didn't want to frighten her.

'I thought I saw something in the water beneath the

boat, but I expect it was just a shadow or a rock.'

'Perhaps not,' he said. 'It could have been a living thing. Yesterday, I came across a creature trapped amongst the rocks, and when I freed it, it swam out to sea. Then a much larger animal appeared, which I took to be its mother. I didn't mention it, as I didn't want to frighten you. Although it didn't seem to want to harm me.'

Eira stared at her father in amazement. 'So there are other living things in the sea after all,' she gasped. 'Why haven't we seen them before? How could this be?'

'I think that perhaps things are changing, and this is a sign of that change. But it is indeed a mystery, and we can only wonder at it,' Adil replied. He too was at a loss to explain the appearance of the mysterious sea creatures, but he felt their presence could only be a good thing. And he hoped that in time all would be made clear to them.

'Now I want to show you another great mystery,' Adil said, indicating the path to the back of the great cavern and the passageway that led to the crystal caves. They felt their way down the darkened tunnel which sloped slightly uphill, until a faint glow began to illuminate the walls.

'What is causing this light?' Eira asked her father.

'We are coming to the first cave, which is lit by crystals. They shine and somehow reflect the minutest particles of light in a most beautiful and mysterious way,' he replied. At that moment, they reached the end of the tunnel which opened out into another vast cavern, but this one was lined almost completely with glittering crystals. Each crystal gave off a faint glow which collectively lit the whole cavern as brightly as daylight. Eira was enchanted. She could not believe her eyes.

'Oh, Father!' she exclaimed in delight. 'This is the most beautiful thing that I have ever seen. Thank you so much for bringing me here.'

'Yes,' her father replied, 'it is beautiful, isn't it? But it is only a small part of the wonders this place conceals. What I am about to show you is a great mystery, which I have puzzled over for a long time but can find no answer. Perhaps, my dear, you are the one who holds the key to this riddle. Come, we must go further, into the next cave.'

Together they made their way through the great cavern of crystal, and as they walked Eira craned her neck to look up at the roof of the cave, as this too was lined with the luminous rock. 'It is like walking on the inside of a glittering jewel,' she said, turning to her father. 'Why is it here, hidden from sight? Such a thing of beauty should be for all to see.'

Adil paused for a moment before replying. 'It is a mystery I agree, but I will answer you in this way: Some things are beautiful only if they remain a mystery. That is to say, they need to be protected, so that their beauty and mystery can be preserved, and I think that perhaps this is one of those things. Indeed, what I am about to show you is yet another of those precious things that are not meant to be seen by everyone.'

Adil guided his daughter towards the glittering, white pillars near the back of the cave, where he knew that the first drawing was hidden. Threading their way between the glistening columns, Eira put out her hand to touch their cool, wet smoothness and marvel at their strange shapes. Stumbling, as they picked their way over the loose rocks between the shining columns, they finally reached the place Adil had been looking for. The glow emitted by the crystals was fainter here, and their light caused the great columns to cast eerie shadows that resembled the hunched figures of people grouped around the back of the cave. Then they saw it. The figure of a man looking out over the cave, as if he were searching for something, the strange horned animal by his side.

For one brief moment, Adil thought that his daughter was about to faint, as she gasped and staggered backwards, almost losing her balance. He put out his arms to catch her, but she recovered herself and stood looking up at the figure, her eyes wide with amazement. There were tears running down her cheeks, and her mouth moved soundlessly, as if she were speaking to someone, someone he could not see. Smiling faintly, she turned to him and said, 'It's him, Father, it's him; I just know it is. It's the stranger in the forest. The man from my dreams. Although I could not see his face clearly then, I am certain. I know in my heart that it is him. But how does he come to be here, painted on this wall deep beneath the earth?'

'My dear, that is a question that I only wish I could answer, but I cannot. I do not know. Perhaps he was painted by people wiser than us, who had knowledge of the times to come and wanted to pass that knowledge on to those who came after them. But there is something else that you must see, something even more mysterious than this, and, I beg you, have courage, for I fear that it will shake you to your very core. To see it, we must go further, deeper into yet another cave. Come, we do not have much time, as we must return to the boat before the tide changes, so that we are back in our own cove before darkness falls.'

Feeling his way along the side wall of the cavern, Adil found the opening to the passageway leading to the next cave. Taking his daughter's hand, he led her down the dark tunnel, for there were no crystals here, and the darkness seemed heavy and oppressive. Finally the passageway ended, and they were standing in a vast cavern whose walls glowed faintly, filling the rocky chamber with a soft, ghostly glow.

Cautiously, they felt their way to the back of the cave. Adil tried to steer a course which avoided the needle sharp rocks that he had encountered yesterday. This way was indeed much smoother; in fact, it looked for all the world as if it had been fashioned by human hands in some long-forgotten time. To his surprise, it led directly to the first picture, the picture of the woman. Eira had gone ahead of him, and by the time he reached the end of the path, she was already gazing up at the painting in astonishment, and he saw that she was holding the amulet. She was looking first at the picture of the woman holding the amulet and then down at the amulet, which she held in her own hand. She did this several times, before turning to her father with a look of bewilderment on her face.

'She looks so like me, Father, doesn't she? And if the man in the other painting is indeed the stranger in my dreams, and I truly believe that he is, then, then…'

and her breath caught in her throat. She could hardly get the words out, as the thought of it almost overwhelmed her. 'This must be me, Father, mustn't it? It's me!'

Adil's eyes filled with tears, and he flung his arms around his daughter and wept. 'Yes, my most precious child, yes, I believe it is.'

And the two of them stood clinging to each other, weeping, until at last Eira said, 'Why, Father, why? I don't understand what is happening. She is holding an amulet which is exactly the same as the one you gave me. Is it the same one? How did it come to be here?'

Silently Adil took his daughter's hand in his and led her behind the great pillar of rock to where the final painting was hidden. 'I think that this is as close to an answer as I can give you,' he said quietly.

They both stood looking up at the two figures for a long time before Eira said softly, 'So it is meant to be. He and I are meant to be together after all. I thought it was just a dream, but it is not. It is clearly written here for all to see. He too holds an amulet, which is the exact twin of the one that I and the woman in the painting both carry.' As he watched his daughter, Adil thought he perceived a change in her. There was a new authority and dignity in her bearing, but without the slightest hint of arrogance or even an awareness that she held authority. It was a completely natural part of her being. He had seen the same qualities reflected in the picture of the man. Then, without even thinking about it, he felt himself bowing to her. It seemed to be the most natural thing in the world to do.

When he straightened, he saw his daughter

regarding him with a puzzled expression on her face. 'Father, I don't understand, why are you bowing?'

Adil, who did not know how to answer her, stood gazing in silent wonder at the regal figure of his child standing before him. What could he say to her? His actions had been entirely spontaneous. Perhaps it had been the recognition of an authority greater than his, which now permeated his daughter's whole being. Somehow, the sight of the man she obviously recognised as the mysterious figure from her dreams, and the amulets that the two of them held, had created a connection, which had filled her with new strength. He must try and explain all this to her, try to help her understand what was happening to her. Although she carried this new power within her, she was as yet completely innocent and unaware of it.

'Eira,' he began hesitantly, 'my dear, can you not sense a change in yourself? You recognised the figure in the painting as the man you glimpsed in your dreams, didn't you?'

'Yes,' she nodded slowly. 'I am positive that it is him. I feel it deep within myself. In my heart, there is no doubt.'

Adil continued quietly, 'And you have seen that you both carry identical amulets. Clearly this is a sign, an omen.'

'But I still do not understand how these paintings came to be here, or how I could have dreamt of this man. What is to become of me, Father? What is it that I must do?' Eira cried, her despairing voice causing strange echoes to break the deep silence of their underground hiding place.

Adil's heart went out to his child. How could he help her to bear this huge responsibility? He did not know how to advise her. After all a dream was a dream. How could she make the transition from the world of dreams to this world? But he must give her an answer, however inadequate it might seem. So, choosing his words carefully, he said, 'I think that the connection between you and the stranger has been strengthened by the sight of these paintings, but how you will make the transition from your world to his, wherever that is, I do not know. You can only wait and watch for signs. Perhaps the answer will come to you in a dream. Be patient, my dear Eira, and above all do not be afraid. You are watched over and cared for by a power far greater than your father. I am certain that this will end well for us all, but for now we can only watch and wait.'

With that he turned and began to make his way back through the cave towards the tunnel entrance. It was time for them to return home, as they must catch the tide, so that it would draw them back to their own world. They must leave this place of mystery and unanswered questions and return to the familiar shore of their everyday existence. *At least for the moment*, he thought, *at least for now*.

Eira followed her father, walking as if in a dream. Her thoughts drifted far away in the forest, desperately searching for another glimpse of the elusive stranger. In her mind's eye she could see the face of the man in the painting, and he seemed to be looking at her. She thought she recognised the horned animal standing beside him from her dreams. She had seen similar creatures running through the trees in the distance.

Idly her fingers strayed to the amulet around her neck, and as she touched its smooth surface she felt the same feeling of movement that she had felt that day after the storm. She was sure it was alive, like a living creature, warm and soft beneath her fingers, but she did not dare to look at it for fear of what she might see.

* * *

Today was a good day for visiting the sea, he thought to himself cheerfully. There was a stiff breeze blowing, and he could smell the cool, salt-laden air. It was just after dawn, and he had already breakfasted, feasting on fruit and nuts. He set off at a swift jog, eager to begin his trip. Some of the forest creatures accompanied him for a while, although the smaller ones soon began to tire and were quickly left behind. Only the deer kept pace with him. But when they reached the edge of the trees, they too stopped and would go no further. Timidly sniffing the air, they watched him disappear into the distance, as he raced over the sunlit plain, his feet making a long snake-like trail in the tall grass.

Soon he had the cliff tops in sight. Beyond them the sea stretched to the far horizon, its deep blue surface glittering in the morning sunlight, crested with little, white peaks of foam. He took a deep breath, drinking in the smell of the ocean. Great sea birds wheeled and dived about his head, their plaintive cries filling the air. Clambering nimbly down the cliff face, he was soon on the beach, walking towards the water's edge where it ran gently to and fro on the shore, and he felt with pleasure the warm softness of the sand between his toes. Giant, orange crabs scurried back and forth in search of food, their large pincers working busily.

Gazing far out to sea, he glimpsed a school of dolphins racing through the waves, leaping clean out of the water and high into the air, jumping for sheer joy. Then he remembered the reason he had come to the beach that day. At the base of the cliffs lay some caves, which he had discovered on a previous visit to the sea, but then he had only explored the outermost cave. He knew that there were more caverns beyond it, and he was curious to see what secrets they held. So turning reluctantly away from the ocean, he made his way to where he could see a large, dark opening in the side of the cliff.

Entering the quiet coolness, his feet sliding on the smooth, wet pebbles, he made his way quickly to the back of the cave where there was a small, round opening in the rock. Peering into the inky blackness, his eyes gradually became accustomed to the gloom. He could just make out the rocky surfaces of a narrow tunnel, its walls encrusted with sea shells and long-dead barnacles. Feeling his way carefully along the passage, it was not long before he saw a faint glow ahead of him. Moving more quickly now, he made his way towards the source of the light. He was eager to discover what could be illuminating the tunnel in this way. As he continued down the passage the light became stronger and stronger until, after squeezing through a narrow opening in the rock, he found himself standing in an enormous cavern whose walls were covered in glittering crystals, which illuminated the cave with a clear, white light. He gasped in astonishment and wonder at the sight. He could never have imagined such a place, and to think that it had lain hidden until now. *Why have I not found this place before?* he wondered, looking about him. Perhaps it held further secrets for him to discover, he thought eagerly.

He spent some time wandering around the glittering cave, examining the light-giving crystals that encrusted the rocks, and gradually his exploration took him towards the back of the cave. The floor here was uneven, covered in loose rock and pebbles, and he had to choose his path with care, so it was several minutes before he noticed it. Finally, as he reached the back of the sparkling grotto, he saw a shadowy figure out of the corner of his eye. He jumped, as at first he thought it was another living creature much like him, but, recovering himself, he looked more closely and saw that it was an image on the wall.

Open-mouthed, he put out his hand to touch the picture. He had never seen anything like it before, and at first could not understand what it was. Then he remembered seeing his own reflection in the forest pool. Perhaps this was also a reflection, produced somehow by the glittering surfaces of the cave. But no, it could not be a reflection or a shadow, as when he held his hand against the rocks they did not reflect it back at him. So what could it be, this mysterious likeness of him, for he was sure it was him, as it looked so like his own reflection. It had the same long, dark hair and the face—yes, he was sure that that was his face looking back at him. Then he saw the stag. Looking quickly around him, he could see that there were no deer here in this cave, but there it was on the wall.

Bemused, he sat down in front of the picture of the man and the deer and stared and stared, willing the figures to move, but they did not. For a long time he sat puzzling over them, and then he remembered that he had often drawn the outlines of the other creatures that inhabited the forest with a stick in the wet sand near the river. Perhaps this too was such an outline, but if so, who had drawn it? For he was sure that he had not done so. Were there others like him here in these caves? Again he looked around, a little uneasily this time, but there was no one else here: he was alone.

With a sigh, he rose to his feet and was about to retrace his steps back to the beach, when he caught sight of another opening in the rock. *There must be yet another cave beyond this one*, he thought, *and perhaps the other me's who made this image are hiding there. Maybe if I go to them, they will speak their thoughts to me, and I can speak mine to them.*

The light was dimmer here, and he had to feel his way along the narrow tunnel, which seemed to go on and on, twisting and turning, but eventually he saw a faint glow which gradually shaped itself into an arched opening. Standing upright, for he had had to crouch for much of the way through the tunnel, as the ceiling was quite low with many jutting rocks, he found himself in a vast cavern, the walls of which were also covered in light-giving crystals, although they did not seem to be so bright here. The cave echoed with the sound of dripping water, which ran in rivulets across the floor, and the walls glistened wetly. In one corner, enormous, white columns rose far above his head. Some hung, suspended from the roof like huge, white icicles, nearly touching their upward-growing companions. Running his hands over their glossy surfaces, he marvelled at the variety of fantastic shapes and wondered what had caused them to grow here, like enormous, white plants. Wandering between the columns, he found himself at the back of the cave and looking directly into the eyes of another mysterious image, although this image was most certainly not of him. The being that looked out at him from the rock was somehow softer, its limbs more delicate, more rounded than his, and the long, softly flowing hair fell in gentle waves down its back. But then he caught sight of what the other me, as he called the image, held in its hand. He had never seen anything like it before, and, fascinated, he stood transfixed, staring at the object.

Shining smooth and yellow like the sun, it looked like one of the small lizards that scurried about the forest floor, with its gleaming, green eyes, but it was clearly not an image of a living thing, as he could see that it was still and hard. It must be another kind of likeness, he thought, an image of an image. How strange this seemed, as he had only ever experienced the things around him directly. He was not used to seeing likenesses of them, not being able to sense their presence, feel the warmth and vibrancy of their lives close to his. Who, he wondered, had had the skill to fashion the image and then to copy it onto the rocks in this way? There must be many other me's here to have done all this work, he thought. Perhaps if he explored further he could still find them.

Casting about in the gloom, his gaze fell on what

appeared to be a path made out of small, round pebbles set into the floor of the cavern. It seemed to lead to a dark corner which was surrounded by some of the large, white pillars. Curious, he followed the trail, but no sooner had he passed between the two largest columns, than he was confronted by the forbidding greyness of the cavern wall. Here no crystals shed their light, and the place was heavy with shadow. Disappointed that the path appeared to have led him to a dead end, he shrugged his shoulders resignedly and was about to retrace his steps, when he noticed a tiny point of green light embedded in the middle of the rock face. Then he saw that there were two, and then another and yet another: four in all, like two sets of eyes peering at him in the dark!

The twinkling, green pin pricks seemed to draw him in closer and closer, until he was almost touching the wall, and it was not until then that he saw them. Looking down at him, smiling hand-in-hand, were the images of two of his kind. They appeared to be the same likenesses as the other two drawings he had seen, but here they were together, gazing out at the world, happy and united. He felt something wet on his cheek and realised that water was coming from his eyes and that there was a dull ache in his chest. These were new experiences for him, but he felt sure that they were connected with the images.Somehow they made him feel happy, but at the same time he felt this aching, this longing to be complete, in the same way that these two figures seemed to be united with each other.

Then he saw that the little, green lights were set into two likenesses of the same creature he had seen the being in the last drawing holding. The two figures each held one of the cold, hard creatures in one hand, and with their other hand they held each other. He felt a desperate longing to do the same thing, but there was no one here but him, not even the sounds of the forest around him. Only the steady *drip, drip* of water trickling down the rocks. The silent mountain above seemed to press its whole weight down upon him, until even that vast, underground space seemed oppressive. Then he remembered the mysterious being he had glimpsed through the trees in the forest, and how he had tried to reach it to speak his thoughts out loud to it. Could that be his counterpart, like the one he saw portrayed on the wall here? This was almost more than he could bear. So many questions, and although he asked and asked no answers came. His life up until this moment had been simple; there were no unanswered questions. If he wanted to know something, the knowledge just came; there was no effort, no puzzling; the answers were always there. But now that comforting presence, that feeling of all-knowingness, had deserted him, and he was left with a yawning, empty ache, as if a great hole had opened up inside him. He no longer felt whole; something was missing, but he did not understand what it was. Despondently, he turned and made his way back towards the tunnel entrance. Perhaps, he thought, if he returned to the forest, these feelings would go away and everything would be as it had always been.

* * *

Adil and Eira retraced their steps back through the caves, until they reached the place where their small boat was moored. As she picked her way carefully over some fallen rocks, Eira put out her hand to steady herself, and as she did so she felt an odd roughness beneath her fingers. Studying the wall at the place where her hand had touched it, she could just make out a strange pattern of ridges and circles. She traced the outline that the ridges made with her finger tips, puzzled as to what they might be. Seeing her examining the wall, Adil followed her gaze and saw the faint patterns in the rock.

'What are they, Father?' Eira asked.

Adil looked at the ridges for a few moments before answering. 'If I remember correctly, they are the remains of long-dead creatures and plants, which have become embedded in the rock.'

'They must have been here for a very long time for that to happen,' replied Eira.

'Yes, they are from very ancient times, before even the Before People lived.' Fascinated by the idea of such ancient creatures, Eira began to study the rocks, searching for more patterns. Once she knew what to look for she found dozens more. Some looked like leaves or whole plants, others seemed to be the skeletons of small animals, birds, and fish.

'Long ago there were many different animals and plants here, weren't there?' she asked wistfully. 'Oh, how I would have loved to see them all, flying, swimming, walking, and growing. It must have been such a beautiful place, so full of life.' Her voice faltered, tears welling up in her eyes. She could not bear the thought of what had been lost. It made her heart ache.

Adil put a consoling arm around his daughter and said, 'What is past is past, and we cannot bring it back.But there is hope for the future, now more than ever. Remember what we have just witnessed in the caves; it will give you strength. You are part of the new beginning that we have all been promised. Hold fast to that, and it will carry you through the testing times that are bound to come, before we can all stand in the full light of a clear day and feel the warmth of the sun on our faces. Come, dear, let's go home and see your mother; she will be worried.'

Together they climbed into the tiny craft, and Adil steered them out of the cave and into the current, which caught them and carried them swiftly back towards their landing place. The water was calm, and it bore them gently back to the bay, where they landed the boat and dragged it up the beach to its hiding place under the cliffs. Spurred on by thoughts of home, food, and warmth, they made their way swiftly up the path to the village and Bethan.

Chapter 8

As he walked back through the caves, weaving his way between the vast, white pillars, something shiny caught his eye. Something that shone with the same golden brightness as the sun was sticking out of a small crevice in one of the huge columns. Moving closer, he peered into the crack in the rock, where a smooth object lay wedged inside. At first he could not make out what it was, so he reached into the hole intending to pull the shiny object out, but, with a cry of surprise and alarm, he jumped backwards, as two green eyes peered out at him. What was it? Then he remembered the images of the hard, yellow creatures with the green eyes that he had seen in the wall paintings a few moments ago. He took a deep breath, closed his eyes, and thrust his hand into the space between the rocks once more. His fingers closed around something cold and hard. He pulled, but at first it would not budge, and then suddenly it came loose, causing him to fall backwards and sit down hard on the rocky ground. When he had recovered himself, he looked down at the object that lay in his hand, and his jaw dropped in amazement. It was an exact likeness of the painted images on the cave wall. A small, hard, yellow creature with gleaming, green eyes, but it did not move. It was cold and still. Was it dead? he wondered.

He turned the glowing, yellow object over and over in his hand, but it did not move. Then, as he held it in his palm, it began to feel warm, and he was sure that he could feel it moving. Almost as if it were rotating round and round in circles, gaining momentum all the time, until it was travelling at the most fantastic speed, so fast in fact that it was lost from sight. But when he looked down at it again, the creature lay resting completely motionless in his hand. On closer examination, he saw that there was a thin chain attached to it, and so, puzzled, he put it around his neck. He would take it back to the forest and show it to the other creatures. Perhaps one of them would recognise it as one of their distant cousins, and they might know what language it spoke. As although he could speak to all the living things in the forest, he could not make any sounds that this creature seemed to understand.

* * *

When they reached the cave, Bethan had relit the fire and was roasting ground nuts over it. The warm, nutty smell drifted out of the open door of the cave, and down the path towards the returning pair. As they entered, she looked up frowning with disapproval, obviously trying to look angry, but she was so relieved to see them that her face broke into a smile, and she leapt up and embraced them both.

'Where have you been? When I got home the fire was out, and there was no sign of either of you. Then I remembered your trip in the boat yesterday, Adil, and I fell to thinking that you had both gone out in the boat again and been drowned! The sun is almost setting, and there have been rumours that night stalkers are walking the cliff tops. But thank the Great Guardian no harm came to you.'

Adil regarded his wife fondly and said gently, 'You are right to think that we went out in the boat again, but here we are safe and sound, and no sign of the night stalkers on our way back. There was something important I had to show Eira, and it just could not wait.Time is of the essence now. We cannot delay. It was imperative that she see and understand the signs that I found in the cave, so that she could begin to make sense of what is happening to her, indeed, to all of us.'

Bethan nodded. She understood the importance of their perilous journey only too well, but she couldn't help fearing for the safety of the two people she loved most in the world. Looking closely at Eira's face, she could see a change in her daughter, so she just nodded quietly to herself and said nothing. All would be made clear soon enough.

The little family sat together talking softly, until one by one sleep overcame them, and they lay down by the fire to rest. Eira closed her eyes, and thoughts of the day's experiences ran through her head. She could not get the picture of the man and the woman standing hand-in-hand out of her mind. The more she thought of it, the more vivid it became, until they seemed to be two living, breathing people standing before her, smiling, quietly reassuring, watching over her, but from where she did not know.

* * *

Thin wisps of mist drifted across the cliff tops, and the grey clouds seemed to reach right down to the darkly forbidding sea, which rose and fell restlessly, an occasional breaker, larger than the rest, cresting the cliff edge. Each time the powerful waves lashed the soft, dark rocks, they caused another section of the cliff to fall away and be swallowed by the unrelenting force of the water. Eira wandered along the shore, gazing intently out to sea. She felt an irresistible compulsion to watch for someone or something, but she could not quite remember who or what it was. Her eyes were drawn again and again to the horizon. There was something there, just out of sight, she was sure, but what was it?

Then she saw him, walking close to the water's edge, on the beach below her vantage point. She recognised him immediately as the stranger from the forest, and her heart lurched curiously. Even though she had not seen him this close before, she just knew it was him. Besides, there was no one in her village who looked anything like him. She could see now that he wore no clothes, and his strong limbs were lean and brown, tanned by the sun. His dark hair hung loosely down his back, forming little curls that lifted gently in the sea breeze and blew across his face. He seemed to be deep in thought and did not see her. His head was bowed, looking intently at the ground. The curious thing was that the beach on which he walked was somehow different. The golden sand was strewn with shells, and long strands of green seaweed lay in heaps, washed up by the tide. This was nothing like the beach that she was used to. The sand on her beach was grey and dead, and there were no shells or seaweed drifting in and out on the surf.

She started, as plaintive cries filled the air. Looking down onto the beach again, she saw two huge grey and white birds circling around the man's head, calling to each other as they wheeled and climbed. He looked up, smiling, and spoke gently to them. She did not understand the words he spoke, but the birds obviously did, as they seemed to call out an answer to him and then wheeled away, soaring high into the air above the open sea. He threw back his head and laughed, watching the retreating birds, and as he did so the sunlight glinted on something hanging around his neck. In following the flight of the birds, he had turned in her direction, and she could see the object that he wore quite clearly now. It was the same talisman as the one that hung around her own neck. Stunned, she felt light headed, as she remembered the pictures of the man and the woman in the cave. Both held talismans, the exact match of those that she and the stranger on the beach wore.

Her heart was beating so fast, she thought that it would burst. What could this mean? First the images in the cave and now, here he was, the stranger from the forest, walking along the beach just below her. She must speak to him. Oh, there were so many questions she wanted to ask him. How had he come by his amulet? Where did he come from, and how was it that in his land there were birds and beasts living? There was no time to lose; she must make him see her somehow, or he might be lost to her again. Rushing to the cliff edge, she called out to him, shouting, trying to make herself heard over the sound of the surf breaking onto the beach below.

By this time, he had walked to the far end of the little cove, clambered over an outcrop of rocks, and was about to disappear around the point. Shouting for all she was worth and waving her arms, she tried desperately to attract his attention. Then, to her joy, she saw him hesitate as if he had heard something and half turn in her direction. She shouted again and waved frantically. He shielded his eyes from the sun and peered up at the cliff top where she stood. Again she called, but he did not appear to be able to see her, although he had obviously heard her calling. Disappointment engulfed her as she saw him look once more in her direction, then shrug, puzzled, and turn back to the point and continue clambering over the rocks. She watched helplessly as he disappeared around the promontory.

Desperation seized her, and she searched frantically for a way down the cliffs to the beach. She had to follow him. It was her only hope. She must not lose him this time. Finally, she found a steep, narrow path down to the shore. Strange that she did not remember this path, as she had walked this stretch of beach since she was a little girl. But there was no time to think about that now; she must be quick. Slipping and sliding down the perilous track, she soon felt her feet sinking into the sand of the cove. She set off at a run for the rocky point, where she had seen the man disappear a few moments before. But as she ran, she became aware that the sand was no longer golden. In fact the whole beach was a dull, lifeless grey, and the sea lapped thickly onto the shore, leaving a heavy, oily residue as it receded.

Horror gripped her. But she continued to run until she reached the rocks, and scrambling over them she rounded the point desperately hoping that he would be there, and all would be restored. That the sunshine, the blue sky, the wheeling sea birds, and the golden sand would still be there. But most of all, she wished that he would hear her calling to him, and that this time he would see her and stay. But there was nothing, only the cold, grey emptiness of an endless sea stretching far, far into the distance. Heartbroken, she flung herself down onto the sand and wept, her whole body shaking with great sobs of desolation.

* * *

'Eira, Eira, whatever is the matter? Wake up, child, wake up!' Eira woke to the sound of her mother's voice calling her. 'What ails you? You were weeping and calling to someone in your sleep. You sounded so distressed, I could not bear to leave you a moment longer. I just had to wake you,' her mother said, smoothing her daughter's tousled hair and tut-tutting over her hot forehead, as she had done when Eira was a little girl. 'Did you have a nightmare? Are you ill? You feel very feverish.'

Slowly, Eira opened her eyes and sat up. So it had been a dream after all. But it had all been so real. Yet here she was at home again, her mother fussing over her. And yes, she did feel hot. Perhaps she had caught a chill the previous day out on the sea. Maybe that was why she had dreamt of the beach again and the man with the amulet. She must be delirious! Yes, that was it: she was ill, she thought fiercely to herself. That would explain everything. She had a fever!

She allowed her mother to tuck her up in bed again and watched as she banked the fire high to keep her warm.

'You must stay here and rest today,' Bethan said firmly.

Lying back gratefully, Eira closed her eyes again and sighed. Although she felt sure that her dream had been caused by her illness, she could not help feeling a deep sense of disappointment and loss. He had been so close! Why couldn't he *see* her?

Later that day, her father popped his head around the cave door and smilingly enquired how she was feeling. 'Feeling any better now? Your mother tells me that you had a bad dream. Care to talk about it?' he asked casually.

Eira nodded. She was glad to be able to unburden herself, and her father understood dreams. She felt sure that she would feel better if she told him. Drawing herself up, she rested her head on her elbow and began to recount her dream.

When she had finished, she said, 'I expect it was just a dream caused by the fever, don't you agree, Father?'

Adil, who had remained completely silent, listening to his daughter's tale, looked directly into her eyes and said firmly, 'No, Eira, I do not. Have you learned nothing these last few weeks? Don't you see? The two worlds are drawing closer together.'

'But he could not see me,' Eira interrupted tearfully.

'That is because the worlds are not yet close enough,' Adil said a little impatiently.

'But why could I see *him*?'

'I do not know for sure,' he replied softening, touched by his daughter's distress, 'but I suspect that it depends on which one of you is dreaming. If you are dreaming, then you will see him clearly, and he will only sense your presence; and if he is dreaming, he will see you clearly, and you will merely sense his presence.'

The two fell silent, each busy with their own thoughts. Eira felt confused. On the one hand she seemed to be pulled towards this mysterious other world. But at the same time, she was somehow being prevented from entering it fully and meeting the stranger, who also clearly wished to meet her. On the other hand, her father was telling her that the Wisdom foretold their meeting, and that a great destiny awaited her. She felt like a tiny piece of flotsam floating in the sea, tossed first this way and then that, the currents taking her where they would. She seemed to have no say as to which direction she was going in.

Adil too was bewildered. The events of the last two days had been so momentous that he felt the weight of responsibility heavy on his shoulders. The two worlds were drawing closer together. Eira's latest dream seemed to indicate that that was the case. But he felt the need for more guidance. Perhaps he should take Eira to see the Great Nuntius. Darius would show her some of the writings of the Before People and the Prophecy itself. Indeed, he might have some advice of his own to offer. Adil decided to talk to Bethan that evening. What passed for summer was quickly fading, and they must travel before winter began.

The following morning, Eira woke early feeling much better. Her fever had gone, and she no longer felt that sense of bewilderment that had plagued her so much recently. In fact she was eager to begin the day. Just as she was about to get out of bed and begin dressing, she became aware of two voices speaking in hushed tones at the back of the cave. Her parents were talking earnestly together.

'I wouldn't risk making the journey again so soon if I didn't feel it was absolutely necessary', she heard her father say.

'It's a hard journey even for a grown man, and Eira is not used to travelling such distances,' Bethan replied thoughtfully, 'but she is a brave girl and well able to withstand the hardships of the journey, of that I am sure; and I know that you would not undertake such a trip if you did not feel that it was of the utmost importance. But, Adil dearest, the way is hard, and there are many dangers'. Then, with a sigh of resignation she said, 'If you are determined to go, you should begin at once, before the bad weather sets in.'

Eira felt a thrill of excitement run through her at the prospect of making the journey to see Darius. Her father had told her a great deal about his friend, the Great Nuntius, and she longed to meet him. Besides, he might be able to help her understand her dreams. Sitting bolt upright, she turned to her parents, her eyes shining with excitement, and said, 'We should leave today, Father. I can't wait to meet the Great Nuntius.'

Both her parents looked surprised, and Adil said, 'So you heard, young lady. We thought you were asleep! In that case I do not need to explain to you, do I? We shall begin our journey today, after breakfast. Come now, make haste, gather your things together. There is no time to lose!'

When they had eaten, and packed some food for the journey in a small bag, Adil and Eira said goodbye to Bethan. She stood by the door, wiping the tears from her eyes with the hem of her skirt. Gently, she took Eira in her arms, and held her close. Then, kissing her tenderly on the forehead, she turned to Adil and said, 'I know that you will watch over our daughter well and guard her with your life, but take care, my dearest. It is a dangerous road that the two of you must travel, and I shall not know a moments rest until you are both safely back here and warming yourselves by the fire again. May your journey bear all the fruits that you seek.' And with those words she flung her arms around him, hugging him so fiercely that he could hardly breathe. 'Go now; the sun is rising and you have far to travel today,' she said, giving them both a gentle push towards the door.

The two walked out into the new day and set off up the path to the cliff top. Adil wore an expression of grim determination, as he knew only too well the challenges that lay ahead. Eira's face was alight with eager anticipation of the adventure to come. Turning briefly, they bade Bethan one last farewell, as she stood waving from the doorway, her gaze anxiously following the two retreating figures until they had disappeared beyond the horizon.Setting a quick pace, they strode along the narrow path, away from safety and certainty and into the unknown.

Chapter 9

All that day they walked. The sun was unusually warm, and they could just make out its golden silhouette glowing dully through the dense, grey cloud cover. Adil had been silent all morning, his thoughts occupied with what was to come. He must find a way to prepare Eira as best he could. He had hoped to reach the Plain of the Dead before nightfall, but his daughter could not match his pace, and they had not managed to cover as much ground as he had hoped, so they would have to spend a night in the open. Something that he had wanted to avoid at all costs, as the Noctu prowled the Great Plain during the hours of darkness. Perhaps, he thought grimly, gripping his staff more tightly, they might find some rocks to shelter under, if they were lucky.

Then to his relief, he spotted an outcrop of rocks with a small hollow at the centre, just large enough for them to squeeze into and shelter for the night. It would conceal them from anything that might be prowling around after dark. Although it was a little early to break their journey, he decided that this chance of shelter was too good to miss, and that it was worth the early stop to take advantage of it. Besides, they could easily reach the Plain of the Dead from here by mid morning tomorrow. That would give them most of the day to make the crossing. After all, he had promised Bethan that he would take good care of their daughter, and he did not want to take any unnecessary risks.

Calling to Eira, who had fallen a little way behind, he shouted, 'See that group of rocks over there? That's where we'll make camp tonight. It will serve as a shelter in case of rain,' he added, not wanting to mention any of the greater dangers that might be lurking nearby.

With a sigh of relief, Eira dropped her bundle on the ground outside the rocky shelter. She was tired and her legs ached. She was not used to walking great distances, and it was so hot! Together they untied their packs and took out a little food. They were both famished, as they had not stopped to eat at midday, Adil preferring to push on and make as much progress as they could manage before it got dark.

Feeling more comfortable and a little sleepy, they sat resting. The now cooling sun was just sinking below the horizon, casting long shadows over the barren ground as it disappeared from sight. It was now or never, Adil thought. He must tell Eira about the Plain of the Dead, before it was too late. Reluctantly he took a deep breath and began.

'Eira, you have heard me talk many times of the

Before People, and you know that they destroyed themselves with wars and famine, and that is how the land became as desolate and dead as it is today.'

'Yes, Father, I remember the stories well. They became foolish and greedy, destroying all the living things around them and, in the end, even each other.'

'That is right. But what I have never told you is that at the end there was so little food and water that the people fought each other in a great war, which resulted in the death of nearly every living thing in this world. This last battle took place not far from here; in fact we must cross the place where it happened. It is not a good place, as the echo of that war still lingers there. All that suffering has left an imprint on the land, and even now, after all this time, it is possible to imagine that you hear the cries of the dying. We must walk on the very bones of those long dead people, as they lie unburied upon the ground.'

'Couldn't we go around it?' Eira asked shaken.

'I am afraid that is not possible. The area is so vast that it stretches beyond the known Lived-in-Lands, and it would take us many months to find a way around. We must cross it. There is no other way,' Adil replied, feeling a sudden chill run through his body. 'But we have the amulet and the Prophecy to guide us. We must keep our minds on hope for the future and away from death and destruction. That will keep us safe, I have no doubt. It is despair that calls the voices of the dead. Keep your mind on the beauty of the forest, and the companionship of the mysterious stranger, and all will be well, I promise you.' He took his daughter's hand and squeezed it reassuringly. 'Come, let us rest.

We have a long day ahead tomorrow.'

Together they crawled into the crack between the rocks and made themselves as comfortable as they could.

Eira awoke with a start and, thinking that they had overslept, looked outside the rocky shelter, but it was still dark, and her father lay next to her snoring gently. Something had woken her, but what was it? Slowly she became aware of a strange smell, a damp, musky smell that reminded her of the hidden wet places between rocks and inside caves. But there was something unpleasant about this smell, something that made her feel uneasy. Then she heard it: an odd, dragging sound, as if someone were pulling a heavy load around the base of their rocky hideaway. She froze, listening intently, as the noise continued for several minutes. Then it stopped just as suddenly as it had begun, and silence descended once more. Eira continued to lie absolutely still, not daring to move, straining every sinew to hear the slightest sound, but she could hear nothing. Whatever or whoever had been responsible for the noise must have gone, she decided.

For what seemed like an age, she lay listening for a recurrence of the mysterious noise, but none came; and so after a while she drifted off to sleep again, only to be woken by her father shaking her by the shoulder. The first, pale streaks of dawn were just visible in the sky, and Adil had already folded his blanket and was reaching into his bag for some food for them to eat, before they resumed their journey.

Hastily packing her blanket, Eira ate the food that Adil offered her. Then, between mouthfuls, she said,

'Did you hear that noise in the night, Father?'

'No, I heard nothing,' he replied. 'What kind of noise was it?' he added uneasily.

'A sort of shuffling, dragging sound,' she said, studying her father's face. Adil went white. His blood ran cold at the description of that all-too-familiar sound. 'What is it, Father? You look pale. Are you ill?' Eira enquired anxiously, suddenly concerned for her father. Perhaps he had caught a chill in the night, she thought.

Adil looked at his daughter's trusting face. He did not want to frighten her, but she must know that the Noctu might pose a threat to them, so that she would be on her guard. He cursed himself for a fool. He should have warned her before.

'I have heard that noise before,' he began, 'when I visited Darius last month. And although what I met did me no harm, I could not be certain that, should I meet another of its kind, they would be so merciful.'

'It was a Noctus, wasn't it?' Eira asked softly, a thrill of fear running through her body.

Adil nodded silently. 'Yes, it was, and I believe that that is what you heard last night. Fortunately, we were too well hidden within the rocks for it to detect us, but we must be watchful, as there may be more of them close by. We are safe for now, as they do not walk abroad in the daylight, preferring the dark places to shield their eyes, which are sensitive to even the dim light that we are pleased to call daylight. Come, let us be on our way. If we can cross the Plain of the Dead today, we may well outrun them, as they rarely cross open ground.'

Shouldering their packs, they left their rocky refuge and set out once more. After they had been walking for about an hour, a vast flat plain appeared in the distance. Its surface seemed to reflect the dim sunlight as it glistened a ghostly white.

'What is that?' Eira asked her father, shading her eyes with her hand.

'That is our destination: the Plain of the Dead,' he replied.

'Why does it shine like that?'

Adil drew a deep breath before replying, 'Because the light shines on the bones of the long dead. They are so numerous that they lie to this day upon the surface. There was no one left to bury them in their own time, and now no one mourns them, so they remain where they are as a reminder to us all to care for what we love and not to take life for granted.'

Eira nodded solemnly before saying, 'And so we must walk over their bones?'

'I am afraid so. But they are long past caring, and there is no other way. If they knew why we were making our journey, they would approve, of that I am sure,' he replied.

Looking down, Eira realised that they had almost reached that dreadful place, as her feet began to sink into the glistening whiteness that was the wreckage of the past. Slowly they made their way through the vast charnel house, sometimes sinking up to their knees in the soft ground. It was exhausting work, and they often lost their footing as the ground gave way beneath them, catapulting them into piles of dusty, bleached shards which sent clouds of white ash high into the air.

At last, coughing and spluttering, they came to a place where the ground appeared to be more solid, and long, twisted planks of a cold, smooth material rose high above their heads, breaking the ghostly surface like towering pillars in a dusty, white ocean.

'Let's stop here for a rest,' Adil panted, flinging himself down on what he thought was a smooth, flat rock. As the rock took his weight, it sank below the surface and gradually disappeared from view, opening up a vast crater, taking Adil with it.

Eira rushed to the place where her father had disappeared and peered over the edge. He was nowhere to be seen! Staring into the vast, inky blackness, she called frantically, 'Father, Father, can you hear me? Are you all right?'

There was a long pause, and then, to her relief, she heard his answering call from far below her. 'Yes, I think I'm all right. I landed on something soft. I can't see very much yet, but…' Then there was silence for a few moments, before she heard his excited voice exclaim, 'Oh, my word, I can't believe my eyes! Eira, you must get down here somehow. You have to see this place. How could it have survived for all this time?'

'What is it, Father? What have you found?' she shouted eagerly.

'It's a vast cave, or perhaps it is the remains of what the Before People called a building,' Adil shouted back, 'and its full of pictures and books. Ah, so that is what they looked like!' she heard him exclaim excitedly.

'Father, we can't delay any longer; we have to get you out of there somehow.'

'No, we must study this place first. It is our duty

as Knowers to gather as much knowledge as we can, and besides, we shall be quite safe down here. Try and find a way to climb down. I promise you, when you see what is here, you won't regret it.'

With a sigh of resignation, Eira cast about for a way to reach her father. After about half an hour of searching, accompanied by increasingly impatient cries from her father, her eyes lit on something coiled in a pile on the opposite side of the pit. Skirting cautiously around the perimeter, she found that it was a length of metal loops, all interlinked, so that it formed one long piece. If she could find something to attach it to, she thought, she could climb down into the hole. Looking around, she found a long, stout piece of metal sticking out of the ground, and, when she pulled on it, it would not budge, so it should be safe enough to secure the metal rope to, she decided.

Threading the links around the base of the girder, she threw the rest of the metal rope over the edge of the crater and began to lower herself carefully into the impenetrable blackness. After several minutes of descent she had not reached the bottom, and she began to fear that the chain would be too short. Suddenly her foot brushed against something hard, and feeling cautiously to be sure of her footing, she breathed a sigh of relief as she found herself standing on solid ground once more.She peered around the crater, but there was no sign of her father.

'Father, where are you? I have reached the bottom, but I can't see you,' she called.

A familiar voice came floating back to her from deep beneath what appeared to be a pile of debris.

'I'm here, behind this large pile of rubble. Feel your way to the right of it, and keep your hand on it to guide you. If you go around it, you'll soon be able to see where you're going, as there must be some daylight getting through from the surface. You'll be able to find your way from there. Just follow the sound of my voice, and I'll guide you.'

Following her father's instructions, Eira felt her way gingerly around the mountain of wood and stones, until she saw a glimmer of daylight. Now she could move more quickly, and she heard her father calling to her from the distant corner of what appeared to be a large cave.

'That's it, come over this way, and mind where you put your feet, as there are all sorts of things on the floor.'

In the dim light, Eira could just make out the outlines of piles of books, small figurines, baskets, cloth and a myriad of other, unidentifiable objects lying amongst the rubble. Lightly, she stepped over these mysterious treasures from the past, and then, to her relief, she saw her father standing in front of a large stone cube. He was running his hands over its smooth surface, and studying some symbols which had been carved into its side.

'What is it?' she asked, staring at the huge ivory-coloured stone block, which seemed to glow faintly in the dim light.

'I don't know,' her father replied as he continued to study the symbols, 'but I think this is what they used to call writing. It is similar to the markings in the books which we have at the Sanctuary, the ones that belonged to the Before People. I think that I can make out some of the words: "Preserve... beauty... from destruction. A place of safety... watch over what is left. Wait for the circle to be completed... another turn of the spiral..."' he read slowly. 'It's difficult to make out all the words, as they appear to have been written a little differently to the ones I have seen before, but it seems that this was a sanctuary of some sort. A place where they hoped to keep certain important items safe. Let's look around and see if we can discover more about this place and the people who built it,' he continued eagerly.

Adil began to pick over some of the rubbish, which was lying in heaps on the floor. Muttering enthusiastically to himself, he started to separate one or two items of particular interest from the rubble. Finally, he straightened up and looked down at the small pile with a smile of satisfaction. 'Come and look at these', he said triumphantly.

Eira, who had been waiting patiently for her father, not quite understanding the significance of their find, squatted down beside him as he picked up the first of the items he had found. It was a small, flat, oblong-shaped object, which had some sort of coloured drawing on one side of it, now badly faded and covered in dust and dirt, but still recognisable as the picture of a group of people.

'This', her father said, holding it up to the light, 'is a picture of the Before People! They looked just like us. Although their clothing is a little strange to our eyes, they seem to have been of the same race as ourselves. The appearance of the Before People has always been the subject of much speculation amongst the Knowers, as we had no pictorial record of them. Until now that is! Darius will be delighted to see their likenesses at last. Somehow it brings them closer, knowing what they looked like.'

The next item that he picked up was a small model of an animal. 'I believe that this creature was called a "horse",' he said, studying it closely. 'What a handsome creature it must have been! I think I am correct in saying that the Before People used to ride on the backs of these creatures, so they must have been quite large.' Warming to his task, he turned to a small, black, metal box, and, opening it carefully, examined the contents. Eira peered over her father's shoulder to see what the box contained. Inside were hundreds of tiny, brown specs, each one a minute but perfect sphere. Underneath them lay a white sheet of soft material, which on examination proved to have the same symbols written on it as those that appeared on the stone block.

'What are they?' Eira asked, intrigued.

'I think they are seeds,' Adil replied, tears welling up in his eyes and running freely down his cheeks. Carefully, he opened the folded, white material, and hesitantly he read what was written there.

These are the seeds of the food crop wheat and the fruit-bearing apple tree. To whomsoever shall find this inestimable treasure, let him plant them in the earth, tend them, and watch them grow. Let him not neglect them but gather the seeds of their children. Eat what they will give you when they are full grown, and be thankful. We who have gone before you did not learn from our mistakes in time. But at this eleventh hour we have tried to preserve some of the little that is left, for those who may come after us.

Reverently, Adil folded the thin, white sheet, and placed it beneath the seeds once more. 'They did not come in time to plant these tiny capsules of life and hope,' he sighed, 'and we have arrived too late. The earth is barren and cannot nourish them anymore,' and he put his head in his hands and wept, great loud bellows of pain and anguish.

Eira put a consoling arm around her father's shoulders and said, 'But we are not too late. It is never too late. There is still hope; I feel it.'

Adil looked up at his daughter's face shining with happiness and a new understanding and said, 'You have to believe it, Eira. All hope rests with you. You must believe it. You were born to carry the seed of hope for us all.'

'I know that now,' she said softly. 'When I saw the seeds, I knew that I must believe, because that is what will carry me safely between this world and that of my dreams. It is what will draw the two together, so that the stranger and I can meet and finally be united.'

Adil nodded solemnly, again feeling the urge to kneel before his daughter, who appeared to him like a regal princess, totally in command of herself and her destiny and yet completely surrendered to that which had guided her to this point, and which would yet take her far beyond it to a place he could not even begin to imagine.

'Come, Father,' she said, 'let's see what other

treasures we can find here.'

Recovering himself, Adil began to search around for other reminders of the Before People, until a piercing scream froze him to the spot. Turning, he saw Eira pointing and staring wildly at a large bundle of what appeared to be rags, lying in a darkened corner of the room. 'It… it's a person,' she stammered, 'or at least what is left of one.'

Adil walked over to the dusty bundle and turned it over, only to be confronted by the ivory whiteness of a human skull, staring blankly back at him through empty sockets. Dropping the bundle and jumping back in alarm, he quickly recovered himself and returned to examine the body of this long-dead ancestor. Searching around, he found several more bodies, all huddled together, some half buried in rubble.

'Perhaps they were hiding here when the building collapsed,' Eira wondered.

'Yes, you could be right,' her father agreed as he bent to study the clothing on one of the bodies. It was hard to see, as the cloth had almost completely disintegrated, but there was a little left, enough to make out part of a symbol embroidered on the front of what must have been a long robe. When he realised what he was looking at, he turned to his daughter almost unable to speak, but she had already seen the outline of the golden creature holding its tail in its mouth. It was just possible to make out the glittering, green eyes, and she too was speechless.

They both stood, staring down at the symbol, unable to move. The implications of what they had found were overwhelming. But gradually the questions started to come, flooding their minds like a tidal wave. How did it come to be here in this place? Was it the Before People who had made the amulet that Darius had given to Eira? What of the pictures of the amulets in the caves? They were much older than this place, and what it contained. This was the third place that the amulets had been found. How were the three connected?

Their minds reeling, they sat in silence for some time, until Adil, his attention caught by the lengthening shadows, exclaimed in surprise and alarm, 'We have been here too long. The sun is beginning to set. We cannot go any further today, so we must remain here tonight.'

Looking apprehensively over her shoulder into the dark corner where the vague outlines of the huddled corpses were just visible in the failing light, Eira nodded in agreement. 'Yes, I suppose there is nothing else for it. We shall have to sleep here, but could we at least go to the other side of the room, away from… them?'

Adil followed his daughter's gaze over to the shadowy corner, and his expression softened. 'Yes, of course. Let's find a cosy little spot over there where there is more light,' he said kindly. Although the remains of those unfortunate ones could do them no harm, he understood his daughter's feelings. To share one's sleeping quarters with the dead was not an easy thing for anyone to do.

Fortunately, Adil had been carrying his bag when he had fallen into the remains of the ancient building, and Eira had had the presence of mind to throw hers down before her as she descended on the metal rope, so they had their blankets with them. Wearily, they found a cosy corner on the far side of the ruined structure and settled themselves down for the night. They lay watching the last rays of light fade into darkness and the long shadows, which the wrecked walls of the ancient building had cast, disappear. Sleep evaded them though, as they both felt a little uneasy in this strange place so full of memories of the past.

Tossing and turning, Eira could not get the ragged remains of the embroidered amulet out of her mind. How had it come to be here? Perhaps the bodies they had found were the remains of Knowers who had come here to guard what their people had held to be sacred. Then she remembered the words that her father had read out to her from the seed box. They had held the natural world to be sacred but had discovered this too late, when everything was all but destroyed. This place was a final attempt to preserve something for the future and perhaps, also, to serve as a warning to the people who might come after them, so that they would not make the same mistakes. Slowly her eyes closed in sleep, and without realising it she rested her hand on the amulet that hung around her neck.

* * *

He could not remember ever having felt so relieved to be back amongst the trees as he did now. His journey to the coast had had a most unsettling effect on him. He could not get the images of the ones that looked like him, which he had seen painted on the walls of the cave, out of his mind. Particularly the smaller one.

For some reason it disturbed him profoundly, and this puzzled him. Why should he feel so lonely and empty when he thought of this picture? It was almost as if it were reaching out to him. And then there was that strange experience on the beach. He was sure he had heard someone calling out to him, but try as he might he could not see where the voice was coming from. Was he imagining it, or had there really been someone there? Then he remembered the amulet hanging around his neck, and putting up his hand to feel its smooth hardness he frowned, remembering that the two images in the cave were also wearing likenesses of the same amulet.

As he walked deep in thought beneath the first sheltering branches of his woodland home, two young deer came bounding up to greet him, pushing their soft, velvet muzzles into his hands and throwing back their heads, encouraging him to stroke and pet them. For a moment he forgot his strange experiences on the beach as he laughed at their antics, speaking gently to them in a way that only the deer could understand. Then, suddenly, he was surrounded by a whole herd of the playful creatures, capering and trotting with him as he walked deeper and deeper into the forest.

Realising that he was hungry, he began to search for some fruit-bearing trees. He knew that he would find a great many different varieties of such trees in this part of the forest. Ah, there was his favourite! A medium-sized tree, covered in small, round, red fruits growing together in large clusters. He reached up and picked a handful, putting a small bunch straight into his mouth. They exploded with a tart sweetness, which made him blink. Sitting down under the tree with his back resting against the trunk, he ate his fill. Several small creatures crept up to sit beside him as he ate, until, by the time he had finished, he was surrounded by a large gathering of furry companions, all chattering and calling to each in their own fashion.

Wiping his lips clean of the sweet juice left by his meal of fruit, he suddenly felt tired. It had been a long day after all, and the sun was sinking below the horizon. Soon it would be dark. He should sleep now. Tomorrow was another day, and perhaps today's events would seem a little clearer in the morning. The creatures who had joined him whilst he ate snuggled up close beside him, and lulled by the twilight sounds of the forest all were soon fast asleep.

It was night, and he was walking through the forest, the trees silhouetted against the gently glowing sky. A full moon cast its pale blue light upon the woods, so that all was lit almost as brightly as the day. He could make out the path quite clearly and strode along at a good pace, as he seemed to be in a hurry. He felt he had to reach the edge of the forest before daybreak, as someone or something was waiting for him there. As the trees began to thin out, he glimpsed a shadowy figure sitting on the grass, gazing out across the moonlit meadow which sloped down to the sea.

Curiosity spurred him on, and he quickened his pace. He was eager to see the one who sat waiting for him, for he was sure that was why they were there. As he approached the figure he slowed his pace, as he did not want to startle this mysterious stranger. But as he drew closer, he inadvertently stepped on a small, dry twig, which broke with a resounding snap. The sound seemed magnified in the quiet stillness of the night, and the stranger stiffened and whirled around to face him. Both stepped back in alarm, staring into each other's eyes, both posing the same question: 'Who are you?' He realised that he had spoken the thought out loud, and so had the stranger.

Both stood studying one another for several minutes, before the stranger spoke. 'I am Eira, and I have seen you many times, running through the forest and on the beach. I have called to you again and again, but you did not hear me'. He looked at the gentle creature who spoke its thoughts so softly to him, and somehow he felt comforted, for he knew that this was the one he had longed to meet. It looked so like the other figure in the painting that he had seen in the cave, and then he remembered the strange golden beasts that hung around the necks of the two figures in the painting. That surely would be a sign that this was indeed the one he was looking for. The one who would make him feel complete, and there it was! It was wearing an exact copy of the mysterious, green-eyed creature that hung so still around his own neck.

At that very moment, Eira also saw the amulet hanging around the stranger's neck and gasped. She too was remembering the images of the man and the woman painted on the cave wall, both wearing the same amulets around their necks. 'Who are you?' she asked, staring at him in wonder.

He seemed puzzled. 'I am the One who walks in the forest, guardian of all that grows, walks, crawls, or flies. Guardian of the water and of the soil that

137

nurtures all growing things. There is not a bird that flies, nor an animal that walks or climbs that I do not know. I know their calls and their songs, and when I speak my thoughts out loud to them, they listen, for I am their master. But there is one thing that I do not know or understand. They are all two. They are male and female; they mate and bear young. I am only one. I have no mate. Up until this moment, I have felt no need of one, but when I look upon you, I feel differently. Eira, for that is what you have called yourself, I see that you are different from me but also the same. The male and female deer are different from each other and yet the same. The stag has great horns and stands much higher at the shoulder, whereas the female is smaller and more gentle. The birds that roost in the trees differ by their plumage. The male is decked with brightly coloured feathers which he uses to delight his mate, and she is brown, so that she might hide in her nest and not be discovered. So it is with you and me. We, too, are the same yet somehow different,' and he looked at her tenderly. 'Could it be that we, too, are male and female?'

Eira looked at him, tears pricking her eyes. 'In the world that I come from, there are indeed males and females of our kind. We are called "men" and "women", and I look at you, and I see that you are indeed a man. Are you alone in this beautiful world of yours? Are there no others like yourself?'

'I have never seen or heard of another, for I am one, until this moment that is. Now I am two but still one, as we are one together.' With these words he put out his arm, intending to take her hand in his, but before they could touch a strange mist began to drift up from the ground. Quickly it thickened, until the pair were hidden from each other, both wrapped in the deepening cloud. They called desperately to one another, but there was no answer. Gradually even the sound of their voices faded away, and there was silence.

* * *

A small bird was serenading the new dawn as he opened his eyes. The sun was rising over the trees, and the first insects had taken flight, buzzing and droning as they began the business of the day. The rich smell of blossom drifted through the air, and he could hear the gentle plop of fish jumping in a stream nearby.

Puzzled, he sat up and saw that he was still lying under the same fruit tree where he had fallen asleep the night before. So, it must have been a dream, but it was, oh, so vivid! He was convinced that it had been real. He began to go over every detail in his mind. He had met Eira, and now he knew the identity of the elusive figure he had sensed in the forest. It was she, Eira. But why had they been parted so cruelly, when they had found each other at last? He knew from his life here in the forest that everything that existed had a purpose, and that everything that happened was a part of that purpose.So it must be with his dreams. But it was difficult to accept, as he felt a terrible sense of loneliness, which he had never felt before. He could not stop thinking of Eira. How her beautiful hair cascaded down her back, and how her gentle eyes had watched him with such tenderness. She had spoken her thoughts so kindly to him. They must have been parted for a reason. It was not yet the moment for them to be together. That it would be so eventually, he had no doubt. But for the time being, he must try and bear this terrible sense of loneliness somehow. He sat for a while longer under the trees, wondering if she too had been dreaming and was thinking of him.

* * *

Eira awoke, her pillow wet with tears. There was a terrible feeling of loss in her heart. The stranger was no longer a stranger. The mystery of the enigmatic figure in the woods was solved at last. She remembered how he had looked at her so tenderly and reached to take her hand, but then a strange mist had covered everything, and they had been parted again. Why? She realised with a sudden pang that she did not even know his name! *But perhaps he does not have a name, as he has been alone until now. In that case, I must give him one*, she decided. *But it must be the right name, carefully chosen. Perhaps then, if I can call his name, he will answer me, and we can be together at last*, she thought, hope rising once more in her heart.

Her father was stirring, and there was breakfast to prepare, so she resolved to think more about a name for the stranger whilst they continued their journey. Perhaps there might be some sign or clue along the way that would help her to choose a fitting name. When they had eaten, they took one last look around the ruined building. Peering into another darkened alcove, they discovered a whole library of books, but when they touched the ancient volumes they disintegrated, leaving nothing but a pile of grey dust. 'Such a pity,' Adil said regretfully, shaking his head. 'We could have learned so much by reading them, but they have been here so long that nature has begun to take them back into herself.She is reclaiming the materials that the Before People borrowed from her to fashion them.'

By this time it was full daylight, and Adil was anxious for them to be on their way, but first they had to climb out of the crater. This proved to be no easy task, especially for Adil, who, although still a fit and healthy man, had the aching disease in his arms. But eventually, after much pulling and straining, they managed to haul themselves back onto the surface, and both lay panting, looking up at the grey sky, oblivious, at least for the moment, to what they lay on. Recovering themselves at last, they shouldered their packs and set off once more towards the Sanctuary.

It was hard going, as the path they had chosen seemed to be unusually soft. Again and again they sank almost thigh deep into the grisly debris. All morning they struggled on, until, just as Adil was about to call a stop for them to rest, he spotted the great, rising rock face, constructed by the Before People, which marked the furthest margin of the Plain. Turning to Eira, he asked, 'Can you go on just a little further? We have almost crossed the Plain of the Dead, and, if we can reach that great wall over there, we can rest easy for a while.'

Eira, who was beginning to think that she could go no further, drew a deep breath, and seeing the wall towering over them said, 'Yes, Father, I think I can reach it. Let us continue. It will be a relief to leave this awful place behind us.'

So they struggled on, until at last with a sigh of relief, they found themselves on firm ground once more. The sheer face of the wall was now just a few yards ahead of them. With one final burst of effort, they reached its smooth, brown surface and, with a gasp, collapsed exhausted at its base.

Grey clouds drifted overhead, and a cool breeze blew across the Plain, lifting the dust and forming it into little spirals that whirled and danced over its ivory surface. As they watched, their eyes half closing with weariness, the wind started to blow more strongly. It lifted large pieces of wreckage off the Plain, carrying them some distance, before dropping them again with an eerie clattering sound, its breath whining and whistling through the holes and hollows of that desolate place. Dust stung their eyes, and, try as they might, they could not keep the grit from getting into their mouths. They wrapped cloths around their heads and covered their faces as best they could, but it was no good: their nostrils were full of the noxious substance. Tired though they were, they realised that they must move on, or they would surely suffocate.

Staggering to their feet, they set off again, following the course of the wall. The dust was now so thick that they had to keep one hand on its smooth surface, so that they did not inadvertently wander back onto the Plain and lose their way in the storm. After what seemed like an age to the weary pair, their hands reached into nothingness. They had found the entrance to the tunnel that would take them through the great barrier and out into the sacred country which led to the Sanctuary. Adil shivered as he remembered his last journey through the tunnel and his meeting with the Noctus. But they had no choice. There was no other way. Unless they climbed the mountains that lay to the north, this was the only route to the Sanctuary from this part of the Lived-in-Lands. At least they could rest in the mouth of the tunnel for a while before going through, he thought.

Just as they were about to enter the tunnel, the wind dropped suddenly, and the dust began to settle. Within minutes it was possible to see way out across the Plain again. Adil shielded his eyes, straining for any sign that one of the Noctu might have followed them, but he could see nothing. In fact, he thought, it was very unlikely that they would have followed them during daylight, but one could never be too careful. Taking his daughter's arm, he led her into the tunnel. As the storm had abated, he wanted to pass beneath the great barrier as quickly as possible. There would be plenty of time to rest when they reached the other side.

Slowly, they began to edge their way deeper and deeper into the darkness. The way was difficult, as the path was littered with stones and broken fragments of rock, and the constant trickle of water made it very slippery underfoot. Progress was painfully slow, and the further they got from the light the more nervous and apprehensive Adil became. Sniffing the air, Eira became aware of the same smell she had noticed the night before, when they had sheltered amongst the rocks. It was the smell of decay and of foul dampness.

She shivered. Perhaps one of the creatures her father had talked about was lying in wait for them further along the way. After all, it might still be daylight outside, but in here it was blacker than the darkest night.

The walls of the tunnel closed in around them. Eira felt stifled. She could hardly breath, almost as if all the air had been sucked out of the place. 'How much further is it?' she gasped.

'Ssshhh,' Adil hissed. 'We don't want them to hear us! So far as I can judge we are at the deepest point under the mountain, about half way, I guess, as we have just begun to walk uphill again.'

Feeling a little giddy, Eira put out her hand to steady herself and touched something cold and slimy. Suppressing a scream, she hastily withdrew her hand, but her father had felt her flinch.

'What is it?' he whispered.

'I touched something on the wall. It was cold and slimy,' she replied.

'I expect it was just moss,' said Adil. 'It grows abundantly here in the dark places where there is plenty of moisture. Nothing to worry about,' he added reassuringly, although he knew that his words sounded hollow and uncertain.

Feeling a little easier, they hadn't been going for more than a few minutes when Eira froze, her eyes fixed on two tiny points of light, which seemed to be floating in the air about six inches off the ground. Tugging at her father's sleeve, she whispered urgently, 'Father, Father, can you see them?'

Adil had spotted the tiny lights at about the same moment as his daughter, and he too was rooted to the spot. Sweat trickled down his forehead and onto his upper lip. For a moment or two he fought panic, until it dawned on him that this could not possibly be one of the Noctu; it was far too small. And then he remembered the little animal that had followed him into the tunnel the last time he had been here. *Of course! It must be another one of its kind*, he thought, relieved.

'It's all right,' he whispered to Eira. 'It's just one of the small creatures who live here in the tunnel. I think the Noctu eat them.'

'Ugh!' Eira exclaimed in disgust, but with a sense of relief. As they watched, there was a faint skittering sound, as the little creature slithered away into the impenetrable blackness, and the pair of tiny yellow dots wavered and finally disappeared.

As they walked uphill, the floor of the tunnel became almost dry. The water which flowed constantly through this rocky underpass had formed deep runnels and gullies down the sides of the path, and they were hard pressed not to fall into them in the darkness. But at last they glimpsed a small circle of light ahead. It was the way out of this subterranean passage, back into the daylight. They eagerly quickened their pace. Just a little further and they would be through. Gradually the circle of light grew larger and larger, until there was enough daylight for them to see their way without stumbling and tripping on the rocky ground.

A few moments later and they were out, standing in the open air, breathing deeply, thankful even for the familiar grey mist, which crept and curled around their ankles once more. As they stood, savouring the safety of the daylight, one of the small creatures they had heard in the tunnel slithered busily past them, back into the darkness. As it disappeared into the shadows, there came a loud squeal full of fear and distress— and then silence. The pair looked at each other, wide-eyed with horror, frozen to the spot. Adil was the first to recover, and grabbing Eira by the arm he set off at a brisk pace away from the tunnel. 'Come on, Eira. We must put as much distance between this place and us as we can manage, before it gets dark. It is as I feared: one of the Noctu has been following us. Why it did not attack whilst we were in the tunnel, I cannot imagine, but we must seize our advantage and make haste. Hurry! Run if you can.'

Eira, half sobbing with fear, ran after her father as fast as she could. Was this the same creature that had been watching them whilst they sheltered amongst the rocks the previous night? she wondered. All the stories she had ever heard about the Noctu were of hideous, wild beasts, a parody of humanity, that would viciously attack anyone who was foolish enough to be out after dark, tearing them limb from limb and then, almost certainly, eating their flesh. She shivered with fear and disgust. But if this were true, why had it not killed them in the tunnel? It would have been so easy, there in the dark where they could not see. The creature would have had the advantage. But perhaps it had another motive? Perhaps it did not wish them ill after all. Was it possible that the stories were not true, and that these poor creatures were not so dangerous after all? Fear and danger were good ingredients for any tale, she thought to herself with a wry smile.

For what seemed like an eternity, they walked and

half ran, occasionally casting fearful glances over their shoulder, straining in the gathering gloom to catch sight of what they most feared to see. But there was nothing.No sign of the dreaded shadowy figure, only the silence of descending night. They both began to think that they had imagined it all. The dragging sounds back at the rock, that awful smell—but no, they had both heard the quickly stifled cry of the small beast that had entered the tunnel after them. It was a mystery, and all they could do now was to press on, in the hope that whatever had followed them had tired of its sport and returned to the shadows where it belonged.

By this time they were both exhausted and in desperate need of food and somewhere to rest for the night. Casting around in the failing light, Adil caught sight of a raised area of scrubby grass in the distance. It would provide a little shelter from the wind at least and was probably the best they could hope for on this open plain. They would rest there for the night, and, with luck, reach the Sanctuary by the middle of the following day. Fuelled by hope, he felt his strength return a little, and he called encouragingly to Eira, who was by this time struggling to match her father's pace.

'I see shelter up ahead. We can rest there for the night. Come, only a few more paces now.'

Gratefully, they flung themselves onto the scrub grass that grew in large tufts, the tall blades bent and stained black by the rank mist that enveloped them for most of the time. It cushioned them from the barren rock that formed the area of open ground between the tunnel and the land where the Sanctuary lay. It was unusual to find any living thing here at all, and they marvelled at the sight of these few tufts of blackened grass. But they were too exhausted to give much thought to the possibility of being attacked whilst they slept. They could only hope that the creatures would leave them alone, as there was nowhere else to hide.

The night passed peacefully, and as the sun rose Adil was cheered to see that they had made more progress the previous evening than he had thought. If they kept up a brisk pace this morning, they would reach the Sanctuary in a couple of hours. They had eaten the last of their food the night before, and so it was now imperative they complete their journey that day. He roused Eira with a gentle shake, and soon they were on their way again. After an uneventful night, both felt rested and eager to reach their destination. Darius would give them a warm welcome, and they relished the prospect of a hot meal and a night or two in warmth and safety.

Before long they left the flat plain behind, and the ground began to rise, gradually getting steeper and steeper as they approached the boundary lands that lay around the Sanctuary. Then Eira spotted a large stone, standing tall on the horizon. It was the first outer marker that would guide them along the path to the Sanctuary itself. Soon they would meet the first of the Guardians, who would take them to the Great Nuntius.

As they climbed higher, the wind grew stronger, until by the time they reached the first guide stone it was whistling and roaring around them, dragging at their clothing and whipping their hair into wild streaks, which trailed behind them like banners. Gasping for breath, they stood by the great stone. The ground fell gently away from this point, and they could see a wide path stretching far into the distance, flanked on either side by lines of smaller stones. 'There lies our way,' said Adil, indicating the path between the stones. 'Soon we shall be challenged by the Outer Guardian, and if we answer the challenge to their satisfaction, they will take us to the Great Nuntius.'

The way seemed easy now that their goal was almost in sight, and as the path topped a small rise they caught their first glimpse of the outer stone circle, its white stones bright against the glowering sky.

'At last.' Adil breathed a sigh of relief. 'It won't be long now, my dear,' he said, giving his daughter an encouraging smile. But beneath the smile there was a look of admiration and respect for this young woman. The way had not been easy. During the course of their journey they had met with many dangers, and Eira had faced them all with dignity and courage, despite her obvious fear. She was indeed well chosen for the task ahead, he thought with pride.

As they approached the outer circle, a figure appeared from behind a large standing stone and challenged them. 'This is the Outer Guardian', Adil whispered to Eira. Adil walked up to the young woman, who stood, staff outstretched, and exchanged a few, brief words with her.

Eira saw the Guardian incline her head to her father, then to her consternation the Guardian turned to her, and bowing low said, 'My Lady, Chosen One, you are most welcome here. Allow me to guide you to where the Great Nuntius waits to honour you.' Silently, the pair followed the young Guardian to the inner stone circle that marked the Sanctuary. As they passed, all who saw them bowed low to Eira.

Two great standing stones flanked the entrance to the Sanctuary. Towering above their heads, the craggy, grey surfaces were streaked with semi-precious gems and thin seams of basalt, whose fine threads formed themselves into a delicate tracery of beautifully interwoven patterns and symbols. Eira gazed at them in wonder and was just about to ask her father what they meant, when they saw a man approaching. He walked slowly and with difficulty, as though each step caused him pain. Adil recognised him immediately: it was Darius. Resisting the urge to rush forward and embrace his friend, he bowed respectfully and waited for the Great Nuntius to approach.

Darius regarded them both with a serious expression, but Adil could see that his eyes twinkled with delight. He was overjoyed to see them. Turning to Eira, Darius lowered his eyes and murmured, 'My Lady, Chosen One, we are honoured to welcome you into our Company. This is indeed a joyous day, a day for celebration. One that will be remembered amongst our people for many generations to come.' Then, turning to Adil, he broke into a smile and embraced his friend. 'My dear old friend, how good it is to see you. I did not expect to welcome you again so soon after your last visit. And you bring the Chosen One with you. This is a moment that I could scarce have dreamt would happen in my lifetime—that we should see this day, when all has come full circle once more and the new day dawns! My heart is full of joy.' And tears ran down the old man's cheeks, wetting his long beard until it glistened like silver. Putting his arm around Adil's shoulder, he shepherded the pair to his private quarters. 'You must both be tired and hungry after such a long and difficult journey,' he said kindly.

Once they were inside and the door was safely shut, he turned to Eira and smiled. 'My dear, I am sorry that I had to be so formal, but it was necessary for the Company here to know who you are and to understand the significance of your visit. I do hope that I did not frighten you, as I know that there is much that you do not yet understand. Indeed, it is my dearest wish that whilst you are here with us we can offer you some help and guidance, so that you may better understand the great destiny that awaits you, and which, ultimately, affects us all.'

Eira, who had until this moment remained silent, nodded hesitantly and thanked him for his kindness. Completely bemused by all the unexpected attention, she looked bewildered and pale. Darius gave her an understanding look and said cheerfully, 'Come, let us eat; you will feel a lot better when you have full stomachs. Afterwards we can talk a little. Then, I hope everything will begin to make sense, and you will understand why your presence here amongst us is so important.'

Chapter 10

In the gathering gloom of dusk he stopped, listening intently to the strange and unfamiliar sounds which drifted across the barren ground. To his unaccustomed ear, these sighing sounds, interspersed with staccato grunts that rose and fell in a mysterious cadence, sounded like some wild and fearsome beast. Perhaps it was stalking him in the hope of an easy meal. He must escape—warn the others that there was something terrible walking the land. Then, pausing for a moment, he listened again, and he realised that there was not one but two of these creatures, and dimly in the back of his mind he recognised something familiar in the sounds. Yes, that was it: they were human voices; voices like the voice of the man he had seen in the tunnel, which led from the Plain of the Dead. That voice that had been so full of fear. Curious how the man creature had feared him so, when it was he who feared man. The thought that they might once more enslave his kind terrified him.

Raising his head and sniffing the wind, he detected a strange scent drifting in the air. Oddly dry and sweet, it could only be the man creature and his companion. He must hide! They were coming in this direction, and they would be upon him if he did not hurry. It was almost dark now, and he could see more clearly. Up ahead he spotted an outcrop of rocks. He could hide there, and with luck they would pass by without seeing him. Shuffling awkwardly behind the cairn, he realised to his horror that the human pair had stopped and were examining a crevice in the front of the rocks. It appeared that they intended to spend the night there. Then he remembered humans could not see in the dark as well as he, so they would be unlikely to travel at night. But this was also to his advantage, as they would not see him if he crept quietly away. He could see without difficulty. In fact he was as at home in the dark, as a fish was in water, and could slip past them unnoticed.

Creeping softly away, he headed for the Great Plain. He could easily make the other side before daybreak and return to his home in the tunnel before the sun was up. He was hungry and had hoped to do some hunting out here, where the small creatures ran in abundance, but thoughts of food would have to wait, as he must avoid detection at all costs. He had to protect his own kind from being hunted down and either enslaved or killed by the humans. He knew nothing of what had befallen humanity. Of how the Before People had destroyed almost everything that lived or grew, nor of how they had finally fallen to killing each other, until almost none remained. For it was into this world that he had been born. This world where almost nothing grew, and only a handful of creatures remained. His people had only the most rudimentary knowledge of spoken language, and they had no understanding of the strange marks that the man creatures used to tell their stories, so their own story would have been forgotten, if it had not been for their love of drawing. Indeed, his people were gifted artists, and this was how they preserved their knowledge, deep within the earth. In the darkest caves and caverns they drew their memories, their dreams, and so left the stories of their past for future generations.

He set off at a swift run out across the plain, dodging nimbly through the piles of dust and rubble, avoiding the soft places, where he knew great craters lay beneath, waiting to swallow up the unwary. The first cracks of dawn were appearing on the horizon, and soon it would be light. He must hurry whilst he could still see his way clearly. He longed for the cool, dark dampness of his home.

* * *

Rested and well fed, Eira and her father sat with Darius at a small table on which were spread several large books. The Nuntius indicated some passages in one of the battered volumes to Eira. 'It is written here that the Before People realised only when it was too late that they had destroyed their world. That a certain point in the destruction had been reached, and they could no longer turn back the tide. It was like trying to stop the waves from crashing onto the cliffs: the momentum of change was too great. All they could do,' he said, turning to Adil as he spoke, 'and this is borne out by what you found on the Plain, was to try and save what they could. Books, knowledge of what had happened, seeds for future generations should there be any survivors, and, most important of all, a warning so that the same thing would never happen again. Those who chose, or were chosen, to watch over those last, precious things, would have considered it their sacred duty to remain there until the very end, which, by what you have told me, seems to be confirmed by the way you found them.'

Eira and Adil both nodded thoughtfully. Finding the sacred shrine of the Before People had been an experience neither of them would ever forget. Then Eira remembered a book that she had found in the shrine. It had intrigued and puzzled her, and she had thought at the time that perhaps Darius would be able to make sense of it. Unfortunately, when she had picked it up, intending to take it with her, it had crumbled to dust just as all the other books had done, so she tried to picture in her mind's eye the strange images it contained, which had perplexed her so.

Turning to Darius, she said, 'When I was in the Before Peoples' shrine, I came across a book filled with strange pictures which puzzled me greatly, and I wondered if you might know their meaning.' She began to describe as best she could to the patient and increasingly intrigued Nuntius the pictures she had seen of great metal objects, some of which appeared to be suspended impossibly in mid air, and others which were set on a long, thin ribbon of smooth, flat material. There were hundreds and hundreds of them, and inside she could just make out the forms of the Before People.

When she had finished, Darius hesitated for a moment or two before answering. 'I think, from the way you describe these objects, that they are images of what the Before People called planes and cars. They were all designed to carry people from one place to another. The only difference was that the planes travelled in the air, and the cars travelled on the ground. They also had boats, but of course you are already familiar with this type of conveyance,' and he gave her a wry smile. 'Unfortunately, these devices were partly to blame for the demise of the Before People, because they not only used vast amounts of materials to fashion them, but they produced poisonous gases when they were used. The cars could only run on special surfaces. These had to be built, and the people had to travel to them in order to use these modes of transport. All this took up vast amounts of space, time, and resources. It was also, either directly or indirectly, the cause of many disputes amongst the people. So, although these objects enabled them to travel vast distances very quickly, they polluted the globe and destroyed much of its natural beauty. But the people did not see the problem in time. They were entranced by these handsome machines and paid large sums of money to own the best ones. They were bewitched by their own inventions, and this encouraged greed and selfish behaviour to grow amongst them. The machines played a tragic part in the whole catastrophe, despite the fact that, at the eleventh hour, they saw the problem and tried desperately to introduce alternatives.But they could not free themselves from this ill-fated love affair in time to avert the destruction.'

Eira had listened wide-eyed to Darius's description, stunned by what she heard. Suddenly her mind filled with visions of the huge, cold, metal machines, roaring along the tracks made especially for them. Dreadful, deafening sounds and choking smells, far worse than the perpetually present mist that now covered the ground, filled her head. She put her hands to her ears, as if to ward off the awful din. How could anyone love such noisy, foul-smelling objects as these? she wondered.

'And now', said Darius, turning to Eira with an encouraging smile, 'I would be most honoured if you would relate some of your dreams to us. Your father told me that you dreamt of a stranger who lives in a great forest, and that you walked amongst the trees in your dreams and glimpsed the stranger in the distance, but have been somehow prevented from meeting him.'

Eira had temporarily forgotten the dream she had had whilst they slept in the Before Peoples' shrine. Their journey had been so arduous that she had not had time to think of it until now.

Being careful not to omit any of the details, she began to recount her dreams, starting with the first one on the cliffs and ending with her dream of the previous night. As she finished telling the last of them, tears of longing welled up in her eyes. Her heart ached with a terrible sense of loss. Although she had only glimpsed him in her dreams, she longed desperately to be with this man who called himself the One, Master of the Forest. In her heart, she had resolved to give him a name but had been unable to find one that befitted a man such as he. But now, without understanding how, it seemed as if she had always known his name. He was called Aarush. Like the first rays of the sun that had shone in her dream and that day on the cliff, when for the first time they had all seen the sun blazing warm and bright in all its glory. Now, she felt certain, she really knew him and could call him by name. Something had changed. From now on, things would be different.

When Eira had finished telling her last dream, Darius and Adil remained silent, both moved, not only by the beauty and strange longing that the dreams invoked in them both, but by the tears of this enigmatic young woman, so tender and yet so full of strength. Opening her eyes and turning to the two men, she smiled and said gently, 'I know him now: his name is Aarush. Now that I know his name, I can call him, and we shall be together at last.' As she spoke the stranger's name, she felt the ache in her heart disappear, and it was replaced with a sense of overwhelming joy and exhilaration. So it was all true after all: the dream would become a reality!

'I think', said Darius, wiping a single tear from his weathered cheek, 'that there is no further need for explanations or instruction; Eira has found her own way to the truth. She has no need of our guidance any more. In fact quite the reverse: it is she who will be our guide. The Wisdom has come to her, as it is with the one she calls Aarush. They are the first and the last. We are their children and must follow their lead. Come, the Company of Guardians is waiting to honour you. Let us join them.'

As they stepped outside, all three let out a gasp of amazement, for the sky was no longer a leaden grey, but a clear azure blue, and the sun shed its life-giving warmth onto the ground around them. But the sight that caused them to gape in wonder was that of the hills in the distance. They lay capped by a covering of snow. As they stood transfixed by the sight, small, cold, white flakes of snow began to fall around them, settling on their heads and faces, temporarily blotting out the warmth of the sun and making them shiver. '*When green-leafed tree and snow-clad hill stand together...*' whispered Darius and Adil in unison.

'So it is really happening,' Adil said. Turning to face the stone circle, they saw that the entire Company of Guardians had fallen to their knees and were staring in wonder, as a great shaft of light pierced the space between the largest of the standing stones, illuminating the circle. Rapidly thickening snow covered the whole scene, its glistening surface reflecting the light of the sun. This pristine, snow-covered world shone and sparkled as the refracted light shattered into a thousand different colours, until the whole scene resembled one huge rainbow.

All were still. The snow continued to fall softly, covering their heads and bodies until they resembled ghostly statues, but none felt the cold. All were warmed by the heat of the sun, and yet the snow did not melt.

'Truly, this is the sign that generations of our people

have waited for,' said Darius, weeping openly. 'Now we can only trust, as the future is beyond our doing. The past is forgotten and closed. All that was done in ignorance is forgiven. It has been wiped clean. We are witnessing the birth of a new beginning. Hope has come to live amongst us once more.' As he spoke, he raised his staff above his head, and the snow ceased to fall. Beyond the great stones, a rainbow, bright with colour, arched its way over the entire horizon, filling the sky with a thousand shades.

* * *

He dreamt of a great, white blanket that covered the entire land, the boughs of every tree heavy with its sparkling coldness. Its dazzling whiteness reflecting the light of the sun so brightly that he could scarcely see. It lay upon the ground covering the grass, and the waters of the stream had ceased to flow, transformed into a glassy stillness. What could it be? The land he knew was perpetually warm, the sun always shone, and the trees never ceased to bear fruit. But this mysterious, cold whiteness covered everything, making it hard for the creatures to graze and feed. He could see their tracks clearly displayed in its cold crispness. The sight of it troubled him, and he stirred restlessly in his sleep.

Slowly, he opened his eyes. He had thought he heard someone calling him, but there was no one there. He sat up, rubbing his arms as he felt a strange, damp chill, although the sun was shedding its warmth on the earth. Then he remembered his dream of the strange, white coldness. Looking around, he could see no trace of it. All was fresh and green, deer grazed peacefully close by, and his favourite fruit hung enticingly from a nearby tree. He shivered despite the warmth, and then, in the distance, he caught sight of the arching colours of a rainbow. Forgetting his troubling dream, he gazed at it, lost in its beauty. All was well.

* * *

The whole community spent the rest of the day celebrating. The best of the food was served, and everyone feasted without fear of tomorrow. Somehow, they knew that from now on food would be more plentiful. They danced and sang. These normally quiet and dignified people laughing with joy. Eira and her father were ushered to a place of honour, where they sat with the Great Nuntius, enjoying the festivities. Glancing over at the two beautifully decorated standing stones, Eira thought she caught a glimpse of something moving, but when she looked more closely she could see nothing but the lengthening shadows of evening. She must have been mistaken—but no, there it was again: a shadow passed between the stones, only to vanish as quickly as it had appeared. Curious, she decided to investigate.

The strange patterns on the stones seemed to glow in the failing light. When she turned away and watched them out of the corner of her eye, she could have sworn that they were dancing and swirling. Quickly she turned to look once more, but there was no sign of movement. *It must have been my imagination, a trick of the light*, she told herself. But then, as the light began to fade, she saw right at the centre of a particularly beautiful spiral pattern, two green points of light which seemed to be watching her like a pair of eyes! When she looked more closely, the spiral began to spin around and around, faster and faster, until she could no longer focus on it. It seemed to draw her in, pulling her upwards and into its fantastic dance. She felt dizzy. She was losing her balance, then she was falling— falling down, down, so far down that she thought she would never stop, until suddenly everything went black.

Someone was shouting. The voice was familiar, but for a moment Eira couldn't remember who it was. Then it came to her. It was her father's voice, and he sounded alarmed. What could the matter be? With a groan, she struggled to sit up, and immediately gentle hands were helping and supporting her. Opening her eyes, she looked straight into the kindly face of a female Guardian, who said quietly, 'You have had a terrible shock. Come, let me take you to the Great Nuntius's quarters where you can rest.'

Still confused, Eira nodded and allowed herself to be helped back onto her feet. A short distance beyond the standing stones stood her father and Darius, both were waving their arms threateningly and shouting at something large, which was retreating rapidly into the gathering shadows.

Turning to the Guardian, who still held her arm, she asked 'What has happened? What are my father and the Great Nuntius shouting at?'

The Guardian hesitated before saying, 'I think you had better let your father explain,' and she gently led

Eira back to Darius's quarters, where she helped her onto a low couch to rest. 'There, if you're comfortable, I'll ask your father to come and see you now,' she said, closing the door softly behind her.

Eira lay back on the couch and closed her eyes, but when she did so the strange spiral reappeared, spinning and swirling, threatening to carry her with it again. Quickly, she opened her eyes and found herself looking directly into the concerned face of her father. Darius was standing just behind him, looking equally worried.   Propping herself up on her elbow, Eira asked her father, 'What happened?'

'I was hoping that perhaps you could tell us that,' he replied with a rueful smile.

Eira frowned. 'Well, I remember looking at the patterns on the great standing stones, and I thought I saw them move. Then, when I looked more closely, I saw a pair of green eyes watching me. One of the patterns began to spin, and I started to feel dizzy. Then everything went black.'

'Did you see anyone nearby?' Darius asked, giving her a searching look.

'There was no one,' she began, then hesitantly she added, 'No wait... I did see something. Now I remember. That's why I went over to the stones in the first place, because I thought I saw someone or something walking between them. But when I got there, there was nothing. It must have been a shadow.'

Darius and her father exchanged glances, before Adil said gently, 'Eira my dear, there was something there.It was a Noctus, more commonly known as a night stalker. When you didn't come back to your seat, we came looking for you, and it was then that we found you lying unconscious between the entrance stones with the creature standing over you. It was just about to touch you, but we chased it away before it could do you any harm.'

Without really knowing why, Eira replied, 'Are you sure that it meant to harm me? Perhaps it was trying to help. It could see that I was ill, and it was concerned.'

With a sigh of exasperation, Adil said, 'Eira, daughter, you know as well as I do that these creatures are vicious killers. They are capable of hunting you down mercilessly and attacking without the slightest provocation.'

'But, Father,' she replied, feeling a sudden sense of injustice on the creature's behalf, 'you told me that the creature you met in the tunnel showed you mercy. It did not attack you when it could easily have done so. Indeed, we both know that we were followed on our journey here, but that we were not attacked, even though the creature must have had the advantage many times and could have killed us both with ease.'

Adil regarded his daughter with a mixture of respect and admiration; after all she was right. How could he be so sure that the creature had meant to harm them? The only evidence they had of violence came from the stories the old Knowers told by the winter fires. Perhaps these tales were just that—stories—and these poor creatures had another side to their nature. Perhaps it was they who feared man, he thought with a pang of pity. That they were capable of showing mercy there was now no doubt. Eira was right. One should not automatically believe everything that one was told, especially if there was no proof as to its veracity.

Darius, who had remained silent, watching father and daughter keenly and listening to their discussion, said gravely, 'You know there is more to these creatures than most people know. They are as ancient as the Before People, and they are partly human. I too have heard the stories that the old men tell around the fire, but for the most part at least they are not true, fuelled by fear of the unknown and that which is different.'

'But it is well known that they were bred by the Before People as slaves, and because of this they bear a terrible hatred for mankind even to this day,' Adil protested.

'Indeed, it is correct to say that they came into being because the Before People manipulated the fabric of existence to make them,' continued Darius patiently, 'but they no longer hate the race of men. The memory of that terrible wrong has faded, and, as they have but little spoken language of their own, it has not persisted through the generations. But they do fear us, much as we fear them, because they do not know or understand us, and, yes, they are capable of compassion just as we are. So I would say that they are also capable of evil, again, just as we are; and this is perhaps where the old stories come from. It is, I think, through fear and lack of understanding, one for the other, that only the bad memories have persisted in our stories.'

'How is it that you know so much about the Noctu?' Eira asked.

'It is part of the knowledge which I have the honour to be entrusted with, and which it is my duty to pass on to those who are ready to receive it,' Darius replied. 'There are many things which only a few are given to know,' he added, giving Eira a piercing look.

'Shouldn't we tell the people that they do not need to fear the night stalkers anymore?' she persisted.

'They would not believe us, and besides', Darius said smiling, 'the time is fast approaching when all these secrets will be known openly, and there will be no more fear or suspicion between the two races. Come, there is something I want to show you,' and he motioned for her to sit with him at a nearby table which was piled high with ancient books.

Reaching for a particularly battered volume, Darius opened it carefully and leafed through the pages until he found what he was looking for. Spreading them wide and turning the book so that Eira could see the contents clearly, he passed it to her and said, 'I think you know this painting don't you?'

Eira gasped, for there on the page was the same drawing of the man and the woman that she had seen that day in the cave. The picture was identical, but below it there was some writing which she tried, with difficulty, to decipher: *When green-leafed tree and snow-clad hill stand together there will be an end, and a new beginning. One shall become two, and two shall become one.*

Darius nodded, 'You read the ancient text correctly. Your father has taught you well.'

'I know that this is the Prophecy, as my father taught it to me when I was still a little girl, and yes, this picture is just like the one I saw in the cave. But how did it come to be here in this book?'

Darius thought for a moment, before replying, 'We

think that it is a book about the history of a people even more ancient than the Before People. This volume was written by them, but unfortunately we cannot decipher all the text. The knowledge of it has been lost over the years, but the illustration speaks for itself. It is curious, however, that the Prophecy is written there too, as we thought that the Before People had no knowledge of it. But perhaps it is merely a historical reference, and they discovered the inscription in much the same way as they found the painting in the cave.'

'What were the people like?' Eira asked. 'The ones who painted this picture I mean.'

'We don't know anything about them, I'm afraid. But they must have lived long before the Before People, as there is no direct record of them that we can discover,' Darius replied, and then he hesitated. Should he reveal this secret to Eira? But she was the Chosen One; surely if anyone should know it, it was she. And he thought of the way she had spoken for the Noctu. Yes, it was right and proper that she should know. Slowly, choosing his words with care, he continued, 'But there is something else you should know, although it is not proven, but much points to its veracity. It was thought by the previous Nuntius that it was the Noctu who drew these pictures.'

'But they are ancient—ancient enough to be included in this book written by the Before People,' Eira interjected, puzzled.

Darius nodded, 'Yes that is indeed so, but it was written during the last days of the Before People's civilisation, and we cannot read all the text, so we do not really have a full understanding of how much they knew about the cave paintings.'

'There is something else,' Eira said slowly, not wishing to appear foolish. Perhaps she had only imagined seeing the patterns on the great stones moving. But she felt compelled to tell Darius anyway. 'Just before you and father found me by the stones, I had seen something— something that made me feel so strange. I think that is the reason why I fainted.'

'Go on,' Darius said, half guessing what she was about to say. For he too had seen it, many years ago.

'The patterns etched into the two great standing stones that form the entrance to the Sanctuary,' she continued, 'I think I saw them move.' She cast a quick sideways glance at him to gauge his reaction, but his face was serious, gazing intently at her, and he nodded, encouragingly for her to continue. 'There were two eyes at the centre of the spiral, and I am sure they were looking at me,' she said with a shiver. 'Then the entire pattern began to spin faster and faster, and I could not tear my eyes away from those two, piercing points of light. I felt as if I were being sucked in and up, until I too was part of the swirling, moving spiral. Then everything went black, and the next thing I knew Father was calling me. I am sure that I didn't imagine it,' she added a little defensively.

'No, I do not think that you imagined it,' said Darius gravely. 'Many years ago, when I was a youth recovering from a serious bout of fever, I was standing, studying the patterns on the stones, and I had an experience much the same as the one you describe. When I was found lying senseless beneath the great stones, everyone just assumed that my illness had got the better of me, and I never mentioned it to a soul—until now that is.'

'What do the patterns mean?' Eira asked.

'No one really knows, but they were embedded in the rock by an art long forgotten. Even the Before People did not know it, as the Sanctuary was built long before they lived. It is as if the patterns and symbols are living things, which have somehow joined themselves with the rock that surrounds them. They hold a power to transport those who look upon them in a certain way to another place.'

'Isn't it dangerous to have them there?' asked Eira intrigued. 'Aren't the Guardians afraid of looking at them?'

'No, they only affect those who have already seen beyond the veils of this world,' he said with a faraway look in his eyes.

Eira thought for a moment before she asked Darius, 'What will become of us all now the signs from the Prophecy have begun to appear?'

'My dear, you are the Chosen One, the one who will bring things full circle; if you do not know, how can I hope to answer such a question?'

'But everything that has happened to me has been in the world of dreams. None of it is real. It is true that I have seen the face of the stranger at last, and that now I know his name he is no longer a stranger, but we still exist in different worlds he and I. What hope is there for us to meet in the waking world?'

'I do not know, but I believe the Prophecy. The Wisdom will find a way, of that I am sure. All we can do is wait and trust. We must be ready to act when necessary. We should be vigilant always. Have we not been guided thus far? Come, your father is looking weary; it is time for us all to rest,' said Darius, turning to his old friend who had been sitting in complete silence, listening to the exchange between his daughter and the old Nuntius.

'Yes,' said Adil regretfully, 'we should rest well, for tomorrow we must begin our journey home. Your mother will be missing us, Eira, and the way is long.'

With that Darius left his guests to make themselves comfortable in his quarters, whilst he lodged with the other male Guardians for the night. The two settled themselves down comfortably, and Adil was soon sound asleep. Eira lay tossing and turning, her head full of thoughts of the mysterious race of the Noctu, the symbols on the stones, and most of all she was thinking of Aarush. How she longed to see him again, even if it was only in a dream, and to tell him his name.

* * *

It was cold, so cold in fact that it woke her. To her amazement, she was no longer in Darius's quarters, tucked up cosily in bed, but lying in the open on the cold ground, which was covered in a thick layer of snow.Shivering and bewildered, she sat up and looked around her. She was lying in the centre of the great circle of standing stones that formed the innermost part of the Sanctuary, but there was no sign of the Guardians, her father, or the Great Nuntius. All was still and silent. She was alone.

Getting shakily to her feet, she began to explore,

searching for her father, the Guardians, Darius—anyone. It was so strange: there were no huts near the Sanctuary, no sign that there was anyone here but herself. Shivering, she saw now that the stone circle was surrounded by trees, and the ground, when she scraped away the snow, was covered in grass, and there was other, taller vegetation growing near the trees. Looking up at the sky, she gazed at it in wonder. Although it was night and the sky was dark, no heavy clouds obscured the heavens. It was crystal clear, and she could see, set against the inky blackness, a myriad of twinkling points of light. Stars, she thought, catching her breath. She had never seen stars before, only heard about them in stories told by the Knowers. Oh, they were so beautiful! Great swathes of ethereal light filled with stars covered the entire sky. Half obscured by a group of tall trees, she caught sight of a great, glowing sphere. To her eyes it appeared enormous, shining so brightly through the trees that the light it shed was almost as bright as daylight. Searching her memory, she realised that this must be the moon. When she was a child, she had listened spellbound to the old Knowers' tales of the moon. She had always longed to see it, and now her wish had come true. There it was, shining as brightly as the sun had done that day on the cliff tops.

She stood looking up, enraptured by the beauty of the sky, for a while quite forgetting her loneliness and confusion. Gradually, she became aware that she was no longer alone. There was someone standing close to her, and he too was gazing up at the sky, completely absorbed by the sight. For a moment she froze with fear, not daring to look more closely. She shivered; maybe it was the Noctus who had been seen standing over her earlier that day. Perhaps he had come back to finish what he had intended to do then. Did he want to kill her? Gradually, screwing up her courage, she looked cautiously at the spot where the shadowy figure stood and immediately breathed a sigh of relief, for the figure she saw was human and somehow familiar. It was Aarush! He stood oblivious to the biting cold, despite his nakedness, looking up at the stars with a gentle smile on his face, completely unaware of her presence.

Slowly she stirred, as she did not want to startle him; he seemed so engrossed in his star-gazing. As she moved, the snow beneath her feet made a soft, crunching sound, and Aarush turned in the direction of the noise. When he saw Eira standing there, he stared in amazement, exclaiming, 'It is you, Eira, the one from my dreams! How do you come to be here?'

'I don't know', she replied. 'This is a strange place; cold but beautiful. I have never seen the sky like this before, so full of stars and the moon shining so brightly.'

'I have seen the stars a thousand times and more,' he said, 'but there is something different about them tonight. Their course through the sky is different. They dance a different dance to the one that I know. And these stones: I have never seen them before. Where could they have come from?'

'I know the stones well,' she answered. 'My father brought me here to this place, which we call the Sanctuary, to consult a wise man who lives here. But I awoke to find my father and all our companions gone.

There was snow upon the ground and everything had changed. I was alone, until you came.'

'I was asleep under a tree and the touch of these white flakes woke me,' Aarush said. 'I have seen the earth covered in a white blanket like this only once before, but then it was light, and the sun also shone. Now it is dark and the air is cold; I can feel it biting at my body.'

Eira looked at him in astonishment. 'When did this happen?' she asked, 'Because the very same thing happened here yesterday. The sun shone so brightly, as I have never seen it before, but there was snow falling, and I saw the most beautiful rainbow, bright with so many different colours that I could never have imagined them.'

'I do not know yesterday,' he replied puzzled. 'There is only this day, so I cannot answer your question. But the colours you describe, like an arching tree branch in the sky made of colour and light: is this what you call a rainbow? Because if it is, then I too have seen one when the snow fell and the sun shone. Is it good that we have both seen this thing? Does it make you smile and laugh, like running along the sea shore with the wind in your hair and the sun on your face?'

'Yes,' said Eira, 'I believe it is good that we have both seen these things, and although I have never run along the sea shore as you describe, it does make me smile and laugh, because it gives me hope for the future.'

'What is hope?' he asked.

'Hope is when you feel deep in your heart that all will be well, and things will be as you so desperately want them to be.'

'All is well with me, as it always has been. But since I first dreamt of you, I have begun to know of this wanting things to be, so I too have hope. In this we are one,' he said. 'But I do not understand why these mysterious things give you hope.'

Eira thought for a long time before she answered. How could she explain to Aarush, as he lived alone and his knowledge seemed to come from within himself, not from books or from the wisdom of others as hers did? Hesitantly she began, 'Where I live there are many people, some like you and some like me. Some of them possess knowledge that the others do not have, and we call them Knowers.'

'Where does their knowledge come from?' asked Aarush eagerly.

'It comes from the Knowers who came before them, who passed on what they knew, and from the books we saved from a people who lived before us, called the Before People. In these books there is written much about the world as it used to be, before it was destroyed. Amongst the wisdom that is passed to all the Knowers is something we call the Prophecy, which tells of a time when the earth will be reborn. She will awaken once more and give birth to many living things. But before this happens, there will be signs to guide the people and prepare them for this miraculous event. One of these signs is when snow falls during summer. These things give me hope.'

'But', she continued gravely, 'there is something else, something which above all other things gives me cause for hope, and that is you. I have dreamt of you many times. At first I only caught fleeting glimpses of a distant figure through the trees, but the more I dreamt, the more I longed to meet you and to know you, and the closer you got. Until the last time I dreamt that we met, a mist came down and parted us. Now we are together once more, but I do not know whether we are both dreaming or awake. When I am alone and awake in my own world, I think of you, and my heart aches with longing to be with you again. Somehow, I feel incomplete without you. My people have honoured me today, as they say that the Prophecy tells of a young woman who will meet a stranger who becomes a friend, and when they are finally united the world will change and be fruitful once more. They say I am that woman, and that my dreams of you prove this. Then, when the snow fell and the sun shone, they said this was indeed the sign that the Prophecy foretold, and they celebrated, singing, dancing, and feasting. For they had hope at last.'

She paused for a moment. There was something else, something she desperately wanted to say to him, as it seemed to be of the utmost importance; for they might be parted again at any moment, and the chance would be lost, perhaps forever. She must give the stranger his name, before it was too late. 'When we were last together, I asked you what you were called.'

'I remember', he said, 'that I gave you my answer: that I am One, the Guardian of all creatures and everything that grows. But I also remember that you told me that you are called Eira. Perhaps you wish that I was also called something as beautiful?'

'I have thought so much about it,' Eira replied,

'and it is my dearest wish to give you a gift: the gift of a name by which I may call you. Perhaps then, when we can call each other by name, we will draw one to the other more closely.'

'It is also my dearest wish that you bestow this gift upon me, for I too feel the need of it. Tell me, Eira, what would you call me?'

Reaching out her hand and taking his tenderly in her own, she said, 'My gift to you is the gift you gave to me: the first rays of the sun. You are called Aarush.'

'That is indeed a beautiful name, and I shall treasure it and think of you always.' As he spoke these words, Eira realised to her horror that his voice was fading, and she could no longer feel the warmth of his hand in hers, until where he had stood there was only emptiness and the faint imprint of his feet in the snow. And as she watched, these too gradually faded and disappeared. He was gone.

She let out a howl of despair. 'Why?' Flinging herself to the ground and weeping, she lost all awareness of her surroundings, until finally, wracked with sobs, she fell asleep where she lay.

The next thing she knew, someone was shaking her by the shoulder and calling her name. 'Eira, Eira, wake up, wake up!' It was her father bending over her, looking desperately worried. Bewildered, she slowly opened her eyes and looked around. She was still lying in the centre of the stone circle, but all the snow had gone, and a pale sun shone through a thick layer of grey cloud. It was morning, and Aarush was nowhere to be seen. Everything was back in its place: the huts where the Guardians lived, the Nuntius's quarters, and here was her father looking down at her anxiously. The trees had vanished along with the snow and the sparkling night sky filled with stars. She was back in her own world, and Aarush had gone.

'Child, what are you doing out here alone?' her father asked.

'I don't know. I fell asleep in the Nuntius's quarters last night, but when I woke up I was out here, and it was dark and the ground was covered with snow. Oh, but, Father, you should have seen the sky! It was so beautiful! Clear and full of stars, and I saw the moon too! And he was here: Aarush was here. He was as puzzled as I was. I gave him his name, so now I can call him. But he is gone, and I feel so desperately lonely without him,' she wailed, looking up at her father, expecting him to comfort her as he had always done, but his eyes were fixed on a spot close to where they sat, and his mouth was moving silently. Following his gaze, her eyes widened in amazement, for there growing on the barren ground was a cluster of tiny, purple flowers. And they were growing on the exact spot where she and Aarush had stood together.

'What can this mean?' she asked, breathless.

'Well,' Adil replied, 'it is a good omen, of that I am certain.'

Hurrying over to the spot where the flowers grew, Eira bent down and carefully picked a small handful of the delicate blooms. She was eager to show them to Darius. Perhaps he would know why they had grown here, where no living thing had grown for many generations. As she straightened, Darius appeared, striding towards them. He still held the ceremonial staff which was used to salute the sun and greet the new day. Eira smiled and held out the tiny posy of flowers for him to see, but as she did so they wilted and died before their startled eyes, a sudden gust of wind scattering the tattered remains. Looking down, she saw that the flowers growing at her feet were also wilting. Within moments they had melted into the ground and completely disappeared.

'Did you see them?' she stammered, feeling completely bereft.

'Yes,' he answered gently, 'I saw them. They were really there.'

'But now they are gone, so quickly lost,' she cried, tears running down her cheeks.

'It is a sign of hope for us all', Darius continued. 'Nothing has grown here in living memory, so something so delicate and beautiful appearing on this barren ground, if only for a few fleeting moments, is a sign that the globe is changing. She is stirring back to life, and she has sent us a sign, a sign that we should not give up hope.' Then seeing Eira trembling, he said kindly, 'You are shivering. Come inside and let us breakfast together.' With that Darius held out his arm to steady Eira. As she reached out to take it, some flakes of snow fell from her cloak onto the ground, where they lay for a few, brief moments, before melting into the bare earth.

'So it is true,' her father murmured. 'The worlds are merging.'

When they had eaten, Adil began packing their few belongings into a bag, together with a generous supply of food for the journey, which one of the young

Guardians had brought them. He was a little anxious that Eira might find the journey too much after her experiences of the night before, but she insisted that she was all right, and that they should not delay, as she knew her mother would be missing them. Besides, the journey was long, and she felt an urgent need to return home to be with her people again. To tell them that they should not despair, that there was reason for hope. The world was changing, and all would be well for them soon, although she could not explain how this transformation would come about, and that troubled her. Would they believe her? But she felt compelled to try. Just as the Great Knower had spoken to her father, and although he had questioned his ability to fulfil his task, he had done what was asked of him, and she must do no less.

When they were ready to leave, Darius joined them and thrust a small bundle wrapped in cloth into Eira's hands, saying, 'I would like you to have this, Eira, as I think it is fitting that it should be in your possession. Perhaps if you look upon the images it contains, it may give you inspiration if doubt should trouble you in the days to come. Handle it with care, as the years have made it fragile.'

Carefully, she unfolded the cloth and took out the battered volume that Darius had shown her the previous day. Opening it at the centre page, she looked at the picture of the regal man and woman, gazing out across time, holding the two amulets. Smiling wistfully, she felt a sudden pang of loneliness. Somehow the royal pair— for that is what they were—reminded her of Aarush. Although their time together had been so short, she missed him terribly and longed to see his face and hear his voice once more.

With tears in her eyes, she thanked the old Knower, and, taking his hand tenderly in hers, wished him farewell. 'Will I see you again, most honoured Knower?' she asked. For in the short time that she had known him, she had become very fond of this dignified and wise old man.

'Only the Wisdom knows that,' he replied with a tranquil smile. 'The number of my days is short, but my heart is full of joy. I have gazed upon the face of the Chosen One. She who will complete the circle and give our people hope, and I have seen the words of the Prophecy come true. Who could ask for more than that in any lifetime? I am content.' With that, he turned to bid his old friend Adil goodbye. 'May the Great Guardian keep you safe and speed you on your way.' The two men embraced with a wistful affection, as they both knew that it was unlikely they would meet again in this life.

As the three made their way from Darius's quarters towards the Sacred Way that led from the Sanctuary, down the hill, and on to their homeward path, they saw that all the Guardians had assembled to bid them farewell. One hundred men and women, young and old, stood lining the path, and as the two passed, each one knelt and bowed their head. Although their faces were solemn and respectful, Eira could see that their eyes shone with joy. Hope had returned to the Lived-in-Lands!

Chapter 11

Father and daughter set off down the hill towards the barren lands that led to the tunnel. Both were silent, busy with their own thoughts. Neither had expected to be honoured with such a moving farewell. Adil felt the responsibility of his task weigh heavily upon him. He must not fail; to do so would be unthinkable. Eira, too, was feeling overwhelmed, because for the first time she realised that something extraordinary was happening to her and that it would not only change her life but would shape the future of everyone around her. Until now she had thought of it all as just the hopes and dreams of a young woman lonely for a husband and living in a dying world, whose father had filled her head with legends and stories when she was a child. But now the truth dawned on her. Ever since that last meeting with Aarush in the stone circle, she had known that it was much more than just a dream. There had been so many signs, but still she hadn't believed. How could she have been so stupid! If it hadn't been for the unshakeable belief of her father and Darius, both of whom had helped and supported her with such patience and kindness, goodness knows what might have happened. She would probably have thought herself mad. As it was, the reality of her situation, despite the promise of such happiness and contentment, was almost more than she could bear, and it threatened to overwhelm her. How she wished that Aarush was here with her now. He would know what to do; she was sure of it.

As they drew nearer to the plain, they saw that it was enveloped in a strange green haze.

'Father, why has the plain turned that colour?' Eira asked, puzzled.

Adil narrowed his eyes and looked more closely. 'Perhaps it is the mist. I have never seen it that colour to be sure, but I have not passed this way very often, so it could be a natural occurrence here,' he said doubtfully.

The closer they got, the less like mist the green haze looked, until when they reached the plain they saw that it was covered in short green grass, stretching as far as the eye could see. A slight breeze ruffled the fledgling blades, causing them to bend, giving the impression that the land was covered in a smooth, green skin. There was no sign of the grey mist. Both stood staring at the sight, lost for words.

'Where has it come from?' Eira whispered, not daring to raise her voice, almost as if she feared that if she did so it would break the spell, and the grass would disappear, only to be replaced with the more familiar barren rock and grey mist.

After a while Adil replied, 'I do not know, but it is surely a blessing. I have never, in this waking world at least, seen anything so beautiful!' Laughing, they both ran through the grass, flinging themselves down upon it, rolling in its green sweetness until the fresh scent of it filled their nostrils and they lay on their backs, exhausted and panting, looking up at the sky.

The thick, grey clouds boiled and bubbled overhead, streaking across the sky with unusual speed, until they parted to reveal a tiny patch of blue. At first it was only the minutest square, but little by little it increased in size until it filled half the sky. The pair lay watching this extraordinary sight, fascinated and unable to move, until Eira said dreamily, 'I wonder if mother can see blue sky. I do hope so. It will make her happy. Perhaps there is grass growing on the cliffs too. Wouldn't that be wonderful!' All Adil could do was to nod silently, as he did not trust himself to speak, his heart was so full.

After they had rested a while, drinking in the beauty of their changing world, Adil realised with a jolt that the sun had passed the zenith, and he was anxious for them to reach the tunnel before nightfall. They would spend the night on this side, however, rather than passing through that day as he had originally planned. Helping Eira to her feet, he set a course through the waving, green blanket. Walking was pleasant now, as the air was full of the fragrance of grass, stirred up by their feet. The day was warm, much warmer than Adil could ever remember, and he found himself strolling along, unhurried and relaxed. He no longer feared for their safety. A new peace seemed to flood his entire being, and he smiled softly to himself. Life was good after all. He had always known that this was how it should be.

Soon, almost too soon, Adil thought regretfully, they reached the tunnel entrance. The sun was just beginning to set, and the pair sat with their backs against the warm stone, watching it sink slowly below the horizon. Something that they had never been able to do before, as the sun was usually hidden, revealed only by a thin, yellow patch shining palely through a thick blanket of cloud.

'The air is so warm', Eira sighed contentedly, 'we shan't need the blankets tonight.'

Smiling indulgently at his daughter, Adil replied, 'I have never experienced such warmth before, but it comforts my old bones so much I can no longer feel them aching,' and his hand strayed, unthinking, to rub his swollen joints. But with a start he pulled his hand away, for, instead of the painful swelling that he usually felt, his wrists and knees were smooth and free of pain for the first time in many years. Gasping, he felt again, gripping his wrists fiercely, expecting the pain to return as he did so, but there was nothing, not even the slightest twinge. Tears welled up in his eyes as he stretched his arms out in front of him and gazed upon the arms of a young man: strong, muscular, full of life. Leaping to his feet, he ran up and down the little slope which formed a narrow gully at the base of the wall, shouting with joy and the sheer exhilaration of his returning youth. Eira watched her father with amazement. It would seem that they too were part of the mysterious transformation of their world.

Looking towards his daughter, Adil shouted, 'Look, look, the pain in my wrists has completely gone. I feel like a young man again!'

'And you look like one too!' she shouted back, laughing. Adil clapped his hands to his face, feeling the smooth, young skin beneath his fingers. This could not be: he must be dreaming. Filled with wonder and excitement, fatigue suddenly overwhelmed him, and he flung himself on the ground next to Eira. The sun had finally set, and darkness was falling. They should try and rest now, for they had a long journey ahead of them tomorrow.

Closing his eyes, he tried to sleep, but his mind was full of the day's miraculous events. He felt full of energy and a strange lightness that seemed to cushion him but at the same time ran through him like the crystal-clear water of a mountain stream. Finally, he drifted into a deep, restful sleep and began to dream. He was walking in a green meadow. A profusion of wild flowers grew amongst the dark green grass stems, creating the impression of a beautifully woven carpet, richly decorated with vibrant colours. In the distance he saw the figure of a man walking towards him with a slow, relaxed, easy gait. At first he did not recognise him, but as he drew nearer Adil could make out the strong yet tranquil features of the man he instinctively knew to be Aarush. Aarush raised his hand in greeting, then silently he stretched out his other arm and opened his hand to reveal a few tiny, black seeds. Looking directly into Adil's eyes, he said, 'Take the life that you have found and return it to the earth. Bathe it in life-giving water and watch over it as it grows, for these are the seeds of the future, and they are precious. It is written that the fruits of the last shall be the seeds of the first, and they, in their turn, will also bear the fruit of renewal.' With this he motioned for Adil to take the seeds, and without another word he turned and walked back through the long grass, the scent of wild flowers drifting on the breeze as he went.

Adil stood, motionless, watching the retreating figure until he was out of sight. A sky lark broke suddenly from the fragrant field and, soaring above him, carolled a sweet serenade to the empty horizon.

Adil stirred and opened his eyes. He felt stiff with cold. The fragrant, sunlit field had disappeared, and darkness surrounded him. He must have been dreaming. Then he felt something small and hard in his hand, which he realised he had been holding in a tightly clenched fist, as if he feared he would drop whatever he held. Opening his hand, he saw three small objects barely visible in the darkness. They were seeds! Then thoughts of his dream drifted back into his mind, and, recalling Aarush's words, he gasped. So it can't have been a dream after all. Suddenly, he remembered the seeds he had found in the crater. Feeling in his pocket, he realised that they were no longer there! Perhaps he had put his hand into his pocket whilst he was dreaming and taken them out. Or perhaps he and Aarush had really met as their two realities drifted closer together, like islands floating in the sea, riding the currents of time and space, drawn at one moment together, and then, as the ebb and flow of the waters of time took them, they were once more pulled apart, separate and distant. At least for now, he thought, at least for now.

Eira stirred by his side and enquired sleepily if he was all right. Patting his daughter's shoulder reassuringly, he said, 'I'm fine— just a dream. I'll tell you in the morning. Go back to sleep my dear. Rest well, as you'll need all your strength for the journey tomorrow.' But Adil could not sleep. For the rest of that night he sat turning Aarush's words over and over in his mind. Questions flooded his thoughts. Why were these few blackened seeds so important? How had they found their way from his pocket into his hand? And where should he plant such a precious crop?

* * *

Lifting his head with a jerk and wincing as he felt the tenderness and stiffness in his neck, Adil looked around, feeling dazed. He must have fallen asleep again after all, but where was Eira? There was no sign of her in the sheltering gully where they had spent the night. Feeling a slight stirring of alarm, all thoughts of his dream left him as he ran to the top of the small slope, which ran alongside the towering stone barrier. Noting with a rush of pleasure that he reached the top in a single bound, he looked around for signs of his daughter.

The plain lay before him, green and lush, lit by the first rays of the morning sun, which cast their life-giving warmth onto the ground. He laughed out loud and, lifting his arms, paid homage to the rising sun and to the Great Guardian, Greatest Knower of them all, whose hand he saw in all of this. How could he not? As he stood feasting his eyes on the sight before him, the faint sound of a young voice singing gently drifted across the plain towards him. It must be Eira, he thought, listening intently to gauge the direction of the sound, for he could see nothing but the waving stems of tall grass. He began to make his way slowly to a point where the grass grew particularly high and thick, for it was here that the sound seemed to be coming from.

As he approached, the singing grew louder. Suddenly the grass gave way beneath his feet, causing him to cry out in alarm. He crashed down a steep bank and almost collided with Eira, who was sitting quietly, singing to herself beside a crystal-clear stream, which meandered and trickled its way between narrow banks, feeding the grassy fields with water.

Leaping to her feet with a cry of alarm, she jumped aside to avoid the sliding missile, which careened towards her. When she saw Adil, her look of alarm turned to one of mirth, and she threw back her head and began to laugh. Her laughter was infectious, and soon Adil too was laughing despite his temporary loss of dignity. Looking down at himself, he realised why Eira was laughing. He was covered in mud from head to toe, so that he resembled a life-size clay model. Smiling ruefully, he waded into the stream and washed himself clean of the rapidly hardening mud.

As they sat drying themselves in the warm morning sunshine, Eira explained that she had woken early just after sunrise and, seeing her father sleeping soundly, decided to do some exploring before breakfast. It was then that she had come across the stream, falling, just as Adil had done, down the hidden bank to the water's edge.

'How did the stream come to be here?' she asked, looking enquiringly at her father.

'I don't know. Perhaps the water comes from the melting snows, but I think we should just accept it as part of the wonderful changes we are witnessing—and be grateful.'

Eira nodded thoughtfully. 'I wonder if these things are happening at home too. I do so hope they are. Let's go home, Father.'

Adil nodded in agreement, and they both scrambled up the bank, intending to retrieve their few possessions from the base of the wall and begin the eerie journey back through the tunnel. But just as they reached the top of the grassy bank, they heard a rumbling sound which seemed to be coming from the ground beneath their feet. It started as a low, throaty growl and gradually increased in intensity and volume until it reached an ear-splitting crescendo. They clapped their hands over their ears in a vain attempt to keep the deafening sound at bay. The ground began to shudder and shake, until they could no longer keep their balance, and they fell backwards, tumbling helplessly down the bank, back to where the little stream still gurgled and sang.

Try as they might, they could not reach the top of the river bank, for each time they slipped and swayed their way to the top, a fresh tremor would send them tumbling back to the bottom again, soaking them in water from the now boiling torrent, which the once gentle stream had become. They struggled to the top for a third time. Not daring to stand, they lay on their bellies and peered over the crest of the river bank towards the place where the great wall should have been, only to be greeted by the sight of a mountain of rubble stretching as far as the eye could see. Of the tunnel, there was no sign. It had been buried deep beneath the ruins of the wall.

Tears of horror and frustration filled Eira's eyes. Staring at the mountainous ruin, she said quietly, 'What are we to do? The way is blocked. We can never go home.'

For the first time in his life, Adil felt completely at a loss. What could he tell her? The wall lay in ruins, mountains of debris piled high above their heads, great plumes of dust rising from the still-settling mounds of rock and brick. The situation looked hopeless. It was too unstable to climb over, and the tunnel was lost to them forever. Shaking his head in disbelief, he felt his legs give way under him, and he sank to the ground with a groan of despair. They should have gone through the tunnel last night, as he had originally planned. They had been foolish to linger here. He blamed himself for his lack of judgement, and now they were stranded miles from home. What were they to do?

A warm hand rested on his shoulder, and a gentle voice said, 'Father, don't blame yourself. How could you have known that this would happen? The wall had been here for hundreds, if not thousands, of years, and not a brick had fallen from it. You could not have known that it would be reduced to rubble in a few short moments today. Don't be so hard on yourself.

We will find a way—you'll see. We have come this far, and, with all the wondrous things that have happened, do you think that the Great Guardian would let it end like this? I refuse to believe it.'

'But we have lost the food that Darius gave us for the journey home. How shall we live?' Adil moaned. Taking his large hand firmly in her small, delicate one, Eira tugged him gently to his feet. 'Well, we can't stay here,' she said firmly. 'We must begin to look for a way over the ruins. Perhaps there will be food on the other side,' she added hopefully.

Slowly they began to pick their way through the piles of dusty stones. The ground still trembled with small aftershocks, which caused them to slip and lose their footing on the loose stones.

'Why is the ground shaking like this father?' Eira asked.

'I don't know,' Adil replied. 'But I vaguely remember reading in one of the old texts about something the Before People called earthquakes, when the ground would shake and even split open in places. Perhaps this was an earthquake, although I have never heard the old Knowers speak of them.'

All that day they clambered amongst the ruins of the wall, trying to find a way across, but the rubble was too unstable. When they attempted to climb higher, small piles of brick and rock would become dislodged and cascade downwards in bruising tidal waves, and they had to fling themselves aside to avoid them. 'There must be a way over somewhere', Eira panted breathlessly, as they jumped clear of the latest avalanche. 'Perhaps we should dig for the entrance to the tunnel. It may still be there, hidden by the ruins,' she added, looking hopefully back at the place where the entrance had been.

'I don't think that is possible,' Adil said, shaking his head ruefully. 'Even if we were strong enough to clear the way, judging by the devastation the tunnel would almost certainly have collapsed completely.'

By this time the light was fading, so, tired and weak with hunger, they decided to rest for the night and resume their search for a path that would lead them home at first light. Sliding down the wrecked wall, they found a patch of soft grass sheltered from the wind, and wrapping themselves in their blankets they huddled together. Exhausted, both were soon asleep.

Tap, tap. Adil started out of a deep sleep and listened intently. There it was again. A strange tapping, followed by a faint slithering and the sound of small pieces of rubble being dislodged and running down the piles of fragmented wall with a soft *tick, tick*. He peered into the darkness, willing himself to see whatever was making the noise, hoping that it would prove to be the wind, or a dream, or a small animal—anything but what his heart dreaded most. Somehow he had forgotten the Noctu. The warmth of the sun and the beauty of the burgeoning growth had banished all fear and doubt from his mind. But now, here in the pitch darkness, hungry and with little or no hope of getting home, the dread of these mysterious creatures seized him with renewed intensity.

Reaching across to where Eira lay sleeping soundly, he touched her shoulder gently, but she did not stir. The strange noises had not woken her, he thought with relief. Perhaps he could drive the creature away, if that is what it proved to be, without disturbing her. Then, through the inky blackness, there came a sound which caused Adil, courageous man though he was, to freeze and a thin line of cold, sweaty terror to trickle down his forehead and run unchecked down his chin and onto his chest.

'Respected Knower, Wise Seer...' The voice that addressed him was deep and rough. The words spoken with great effort, as if their form and shape were unfamiliar to the speaker. As Adil did not reply, the voice addressed him again: 'Respected Knower, Wise Seer, do you not understand my words? This form of speech is unfamiliar to me. My father taught me man speech long ago, but I have not uttered a word in your tongue for many long years. Are the words known to you?'

Adil sat peering into the darkness, straining to see who or what was speaking to him. Composing himself as best he could, he replied, 'Yes, I understand your speech. Who addresses me, Adil, Knower of the Lived-in-Lands?'

'My name is Tenebrae,' came the laboured reply, 'leader of the race of Noctu. We know of the Prophecy, and we are honoured to welcome you and your daughter to our land. For as long as we can remember, these lands have lain barren and empty, and we, hunted by humankind, have feared the light of day, only venturing out after dark, even here in our own lands. The very sight of us struck terror into the hearts of your people, so they hated us and called us many vile things. But we are true to the Great Guardian, just as

you are, Adil of the Grey Coast, and we desire to help
you now, so that the Prophecy may be fulfilled. But it
is our wish that you and your fair daughter should not
lay eyes upon us. There will come a time, we are told,
when we shall no longer fear the rays of the sun, or
the revealing light of day, when humankind will gaze
upon us with favour. But those days are not yet with
us. So if you trust my word and will accept our aid, it
can only be given under the sheltering cover of night.'

Adil was silent for a moment. In his heart, he felt
sure that he could trust the owner of the disembodied
voice, but would he be able to convince Eira of his
sincerity? There was only one way to find out, and
besides, what choice did they have? Tenebrae and his
subjects were almost certainly their only hope.

'I for one feel that I can trust you, Tenebrae,' he
replied, 'but I must also convince my daughter to
accept your help.'

He was about to rouse Eira from her sleep, when he
felt a gentle hand on his arm and heard his daughter's
soft voice speaking very close to his ear. 'Father, I feel
that this is the Noctus who came to me in the stone
circle. He has a good heart, and I am certain that we
can rely on his help. Let us go with him, as I am sure
he will be true to his word.'

'How will you guide us Tenebrae?' Adil called out.

In answer to his question, a long staff made of
knotted wood appeared through the darkness. 'Take
hold of this, Knower, and bid your daughter grasp
your hand in her turn. This way shall I lead you,' the
gruff voice replied.

Adil took hold of the wooden stave and gently

placed his daughter's hand in his, whispering encouragingly as he did so. 'Come, Eira, let us delay no longer; we must begin this strange journey. It will be a true lesson in trust for us all.'

Slowly they edged forward, Adil feeling the gentle but firm tug on the other end of the wooden pole, which connected them to their unseen companion and guide. Gradually, little by little, inch by inch, they felt themselves ascending the pile of loose stones. Now and again one of the pair would lose their footing, slipping and sliding down the seemingly endless mountain of rock. Their guide would stop immediately, and, after enquiring about their welfare, wait patiently whilst they struggled their way back up the slippery mound, until they reached the place where the end of the staff lay ready for them to resume their slow and painful progress. But never once did they catch a single glimpse of their companion, nor did he make the slightest sound. The slippery, uneven surfaces seemed to cause him no trouble.

When they had been travelling this way for what seemed like an eternity, Adil called into the darkness, 'Tenebrae, we are tired and must rest. We have neither eaten nor drunk anything since yesterday morning, and we are weak with hunger.'

'Rest then, if you must, but daylight approaches. Progress is slow and we have far to travel. If it is sustenance that you lack, if you will consent to eat the food of my kind, I will willingly share what I have with you. You may not find it to your taste, but it will sustain you until you are able to find food which is more to your liking,' the Noctus replied.

As by now they were both in desperate need of something to eat, Adil agreed to Tenebrae's offer with little hesitation. 'You are very kind, and we gladly accept whatever you are able to spare'.

'Sit then, rest, and close your eyes, both of you, until I speak again,' Tenebrae replied. Obediently the pair complied, reluctantly closing their eyes. Both felt a slight waft of air and the smell of wet leaves and mud, then Tenebrae's voice spoke to them once more from out of the gloom. 'Eat, regain your strength.'

On a smooth rock, a short distance from where they sat, they could just make out the dim outline of a small package. Adil rose and took the bundle, which was damp and cold. The outer wrapping appeared to be made from some sort of tree bark. Opening the parcel, he found four small piles of food. Taking one in his hand, he examined it more closely. It seemed to be composed of small insects, fungi, and some of the ground nuts that his wife and daughter foraged for at home, which formed the basis of their own diet. They were both faint with hunger, and this was not the time to question what they were eating. *Besides,* he thought, *we would not want to offend our host, as he has shared his food so generously with us.* So without saying anything he handed one of the small piles to Eira, hoping that she would not look too closely at what it contained. Hungrily she put it straight into her mouth. He could not see the expression on her face, but he sensed her revulsion. Quickly, before he could think more about it, he popped the second morsel of food into his own mouth. The taste of decay all but overwhelmed him, but somehow he managed to swallow and hand another mouthful to his daughter, whilst finishing the last himself.

'Is our food to your liking, Knower?' asked the voice. 'What you have eaten is a delicacy amongst our people, as the ingredients are hard to find.'

'We are indeed honoured to share such riches with you, Tenebrae, and grateful for your sacrifice,' Adil replied quickly.

'It is well then,' said the Noctus. 'If you and the Honoured One are rested, we should continue our journey, as time is pressing.'

Eira nodded, and signalling their readiness they rose wearily to their feet. They could delay no longer and must heed the urgings of their guide. Already, a few thin streaks of light were visible on the far horizon, and they knew that Tenebrae would not consent to be seen in daylight. Time was of the essence. They must hurry, despite their weariness.

For what seemed like hours, they continued to scramble over the uneven piles of the fallen wall, until their guide called for them to halt. 'There is a way through the wall at this point,' said Tenebrae, his rough voice drifting through the darkness to where they stood. 'My people tunnelled through the rubble yesterday in an effort to shelter from the daylight. The wall must have been thinner at this point, for they soon found themselves on the far side of the ruins. Wait here, for I must call my kin. Not all of them are as kindly disposed to those of the humankind as I am.'

By the time Tenebrae returned to where the exhausted pair waited, shivering with cold and hunger, the sun was already casting a red glow over the distant hills, and they could just make out the shambling figure of the Noctu chieftain as he approached, closely followed by a small group of his kind. 'This way,' he called impatiently to them. 'Hurry, the sun is already beginning his journey through the sky, and we have no wish to feel the stinging barbs of his rays upon our backs.'

Adil grabbed the end of the wooden staff, and they followed Tenebrae as best they could, until a circle of seemingly impenetrable darkness loomed in front of them. As they approached, it seemed to send out long tendrils of misty blackness, which wrapped themselves around the shivering pair, embracing them with icy cold fingers, filled with the smell of dampness and decay. Putting out his free hand, Adil felt the cold sides of a tunnel. Much smaller than the original, it had obviously been constructed in haste, for the walls were rough and uneven.

Tenebrae tugged urgently on the staff. 'Soon you will see the light of the sun. That which fills us with terror and foreboding will warm you and bring you strength,' he said. As he spoke, a thin shaft of light pierced the darkness, casting a tiny, round coin of light on the ground in front of the Noctu leader. With a curse, he stepped quickly aside. 'Here I must leave you, Honoured One, Adil of the Grey Coast. My task is done. When you leave this place, head south, as I have brought you many miles to the north of the old crossing place. May the Great Guardian keep you safe, and if we live to see the Prophecy fulfilled, perhaps we shall meet again, and our two peoples can learn to live together in peace and understanding. Until that day, as my people say, may your tread be sure, and the sight which needs no light be your guide. Farewell.' With these words, Tenebrae and his companions vanished noiselessly into the darkness, leaving the bewildered pair alone in the lightening gloom.

Together they felt their way to the mouth of the tunnel. Pausing at the entrance, they breathed deeply of the fresh morning air, and stared wide-eyed with wonder at the sight which met their eyes. Surely they must be dreaming—this couldn't be real, could it? Gone was the barren, grey rock, devoid of all growing things. Gone was the grey mist which crept along the ground, seeping into every crack and crevice, drenching everything in its foul-smelling dampness. Whilst they were in the tunnel, the sun had risen and was now riding high in a sky of dazzling blue. The ground at their feet was thick with a luxuriant carpet of grass, growing so high that the morning breeze stirred its waving stems, causing it to sway in great currents and eddies of graceful motion, like a green river flowing to the sea. Overhead a great bird wheeled, hanging on the warm currents of moving air that rose from the green landscape below, its long wings outstretched, arcing gracefully through the stillness. Occasionally it would lift its head, emitting a shrill cry.

'It is calling for its mate,' Eira said suddenly. 'Every creature has a companion waiting for it somewhere. I feel it. The world is changing. All things must find their opposite, so that balance can be restored. Then all will be complete and the Prophecy fulfilled.'

As they watched, a second bird appeared, and the two began an aerial dance so filled with grace that both

199

Eira and Adil stood hypnotised by its beauty. Finally, the two birds alighted on a rock not far from where the human pair stood. Calmly they waited whilst father and daughter approached. As they drew nearer, Eira and Adil saw an area of level ground at the base of the great rock on which the birds were perched. The grass grew more sparsely here, and a little spring trickled from a crevice in the rocks.

Eira walked confidently towards the great birds. She showed no fear of them, and they calmly allowed her to approach, cocking their heads to one side, watching her. Turning to her father, she said suddenly, 'We should plant the black seeds here. The birds have shown us the place. The ground is level, warmed by the sun, and there is water.'

Adil took the seeds from his pocket, and as he did so he remembered his dream of Aarush. Recent events had driven it from his mind, so Eira knew nothing of it or Aarush's words. But somehow, guided by the presence of the great birds, she had understood the need to plant the seeds in this place. Without another word, he made a series of small holes in the ground, carefully placing a single seed in each one and covering them with soil. Next, he filled his drinking cup with water from the spring and poured it over the little mounds of earth.

'Now all we can do is wait. I do not know how long it will take for them to grow, as I have no knowledge of such things, but I will send someone from the village to watch over this place until they are safely grown,' he said. 'For now, let us rest a little before we continue our journey.'

Eira nodded and said, 'Yes, when I saw the birds, I just knew that we should plant the seeds here; that this was the right place for them, and that they would be a sign of great hope for the future.'

Both were silent for a while, occupied with their own thoughts, until fatigue overcame them, and they lay down on the warm grass to rest. Watched by their new companions and soothed by the gentle sound of water running down the rocks from the little spring, they were soon asleep.

Exhausted by their adventures, they slept all the rest of that day and through the following night. Adil awoke to the sound of buzzing insects. A fly landed on his face, tickling his cheek. Alarmed, he jumped up staring wildly around him, sensing the passing of much time. How long had they slept? he wondered, confused. Eira was just stirring. She yawned and stretched lazily.

'We must have slept for one whole day and night,' Adil said, frowning. They had wasted enough time already, and with no food it was essential that they reached home as quickly as possible.

Turning to look at his daughter and intending to urge her to make preparations to leave immediately, he saw that she was staring open-mouthed at something. Following her gaze, his eyes widened in astonishment, for growing on the very spot where they had planted the black seeds the day before were three fruit trees, fully grown and covered in sweet-smelling blossom. The air around the trees was thick with bees, attracted to the flowers. As they watched, spellbound, a stiff breeze blew up, blowing all the blossom off the trees in great clouds of pink and white petals, which filled the air like fragrant snowflakes.

Eira sighed with disappointment. 'Oh, what a shame the blossom has gone already. Surely there will be no fruit now.'

Adil, who had been standing speechless, looked regretfully at Eira. 'Yes, I fear you are right, although why would the Great Guardian cause such a miracle as this to happen, only to destroy it before it had come to fruition? I cannot believe that the Greatest Knower would do such a thing. Come, we can bathe in the stream and wait a while. After all, so much time has passed already that a few more hours won't hurt. Let's just wait and see what happens!'

They returned from washing in the spring and drinking the clear water to find the trees covered in fruit. Adil closed his eyes in gratitude and lifted his face to the sky. Tears were running down his cheeks.

Turning to her father, Eira said quietly, 'You knew that this would happen, didn't you, Father?'

'Yes, I dared to hope that it would,' he sighed, his face working with emotion. 'It is one of the signs given in the Prophecy: *When three trees flower and bear fruit before the sun sets, all shall taste of their sweetness once more.*'

Reaching up slowly, almost reverently, Eira cupped her hand around one of the lowest growing fruits. They were round and hard, their green and red skins smooth and shiny to the touch. Gently she tugged, and the fruit came free. For several moments she stood looking down at the small miracle in her hand, hardly daring to believe that it was real, then lifting it cautiously to her lips she took a bite. A crisp, sweet hardness filled her mouth. Chewing slowly, she savoured its delicious unfamiliarity. Swallowing, the first bite was gone, so she took another, then another. Faster and faster she ate as her hunger overtook her, and the firm, juicy fruit seemed to all but overwhelm her with its goodness. Then it was finished, and she turned to her father, eager for him to share this wonder. Stretching up to where a particularly handsome fruit grew, she picked it and handed it to him, urging him to eat.

'Go on, Father, try it; they are truly delicious!' she cried, as her strength returned and happiness flooded her whole being. Everything was going to be all right. She knew it was.

Chapter 12

Fortified by their meal of fruit, the two made reluctant preparations to leave the tiny orchard that had sprung up so miraculously over night. Of the two birds who had guided them to the planting place, there was no sign.

'They have done their work, so now they are attending to their own concerns. I am sure that they have a nest of young ones to rear, although it will take a while to fill this land with their kind,' Eira said. Strangely, she did not think to question where this first pair had come from. The world was so full of magic as her own world and Aarush's drew closer together.

As they walked, Adil recounted his dream of how he had met with Aarush, who had handed him the seeds which he already held in his own pocket and instructed him to plant them, telling him that they would be the fruit of a new beginning.

Eira listened in silence as her father told his story. When he had finished, she began thoughtfully, 'I feel that his world and ours are drawing closer, and all these wonderful events are signs of that, but somehow the two cannot yet remain together. Oh, I do so hope that the time will come very soon, as I cannot bear to be without him any longer,' she cried desperately.

Adil put his arm around his daughter's shoulder, doing his best to soothe her distress. 'Now is not the time for grieving. Our lives are filled with hope. We have come this far; don't give up now! Come, let's see if we can reach home before nightfall. We have lingered too long on the road already, and your mother will begin to think that we are not coming back. Do you suppose there is grass growing there too?' he said smiling encouragingly at her.

When they paused for a brief rest, Eira stood, shading her eyes and scanning the horizon. 'What is that light I can see in the distance?' she asked.

'I think it is the sea,' said Adil. 'The sun must be shining on the water, causing it to reflect the light like a mirror. I have never seen anything like it before,' he added, awestruck by the sight of the glistening radiance.

* * *

The sun was sinking low in the sky by the time they reached the village, but people were still sitting outside. This was almost unknown, as the mist usually drove them to seek shelter by late afternoon. The air was warm, and a stiff breeze blew off the sea, bringing with it the fresh smell of salt and ozone. Great white and grey birds with yellow beaks wheeled and cried overhead, flying low over the shimmering water and high above them along the cliffs. Short, coarse grass grew beneath their feet, and swathes of little violet flowers grew everywhere, making the cliff tops look like one huge, coloured patchwork.

As they approached the cave, a figure came running towards them. It was Bethan. Sobbing hysterically, she threw her arms around Adil's neck, kissing him savagely all over his face. Then turning to Eira, she embraced her with a ferocious joy. 'I thought you were both dead! When you didn't come back, I thought you must have been killed in the great earthquake, and that I would never see you again. But now my happiness is complete. The Great Guardian has brought you back to me, and we can share this miracle together.' Then she took a step backwards, staring at Adil in amazement. 'Adil? Is this truly my Adil? Adil, respected Knower of the Grey Coast, wiseman of many winters? You look as if you have scarcely seen more than twenty!'

He smiled at her, his eyes twinkling with amusement, and replied. 'My dear wife, I suggest you find a clear pool and look at your reflection, as I think you will find that you too are a little changed!'

Bethan's hands flew to her face, and, feeling the smooth skin of a young woman beneath her fingers, she gasped, 'What can this mean?'

'I think', Adil replied thoughtfully, 'that as this world of ours is changing, and we are a part of it, we too are changing.' And they looked at each other tenderly and laughed softly, their eyes brimming with tears. Who could have thought that such a thing was possible?

Seeing the ruins of some of the village houses nearby, Adil enquired, concerned, 'So you felt the earthquake here too?'

'Yes, yes, it shook the ground for two whole days and nights, and some of the houses in the village were destroyed, but, thank the Great Guardian, no one was hurt,' Bethan replied. 'But you and Eira must also have felt the ground shaking?'

'Yes, indeed we did, and the great wall was razed to the ground. We had a lucky escape. The tunnel was blocked, and we were trapped on the other side.'

Bethan gasped in horror and fell silent for a moment, before asking, 'Then how did you find your way back?'

Adil looked fondly at his wife before replying. Oh, how he had missed her gentle presence. 'The Noctu helped us. But it is a long story, and one best told by the fire over a bowl of hot soup,' he added, suddenly aware of how ravenously hungry he was.

Bethan smiled, and holding out her hand to her husband she led him into their rocky shelter, where she busied herself preparing a meal for the weary travellers. Adil sat by the fire watching her dreamily, revelling in the warmth and cheerfulness of its glow and the loving presence of his wife. He was glad to be home.

After her parents had gone in, Eira lingered outside. She wanted to be alone for a while. She needed time to think about the events of the last few days. So much had happened; it was all too much to take in at once.

She turned and watched the last rays of the setting sun dip below the horizon, staring in wonder as first one then another small point of light appeared in the darkening sky, until the heavens were full of tiny lights, which sparkled and danced before her eyes like miniature jewels set in the velvety blackness. 'Stars,' she breathed. 'They are stars.' She remembered her father reading something to her from the Wisdom teachings when she was a little girl. The globe on which they lived revolved around the sun, and although they could not see them because of the deep cloud that enveloped their world, there were many other shining bodies like their sun. In fact, there were so many that you could not count them, and they were spread over distances beyond imagining, filling the heavens with their light. *I wonder if any of them have worlds like ours revolving around them, and if there are people living there*, she mused. A cloud of sadness passed across her face as she thought of Aarush. Perhaps somewhere, he too was looking up at the sky, and she hoped with an aching heart he was thinking of her.

'Eira!' Her mother was calling her. 'Eira, come and eat something!'

Reluctantly, she turned and made her way towards the door, stealing one last look at the luminous sky as she went. She did so hope that the stars would be there again tomorrow night, then she could spend more time studying them.

'Eira,' her mother's voice called impatiently, 'your supper is getting cold!'

'I'm coming mother,' she replied with a wistful sigh.

The following morning Adil rose early, as he was

eager to plant the remainder of the seeds that he had found in the crater. What did the note he had found call them? They were wheat seeds—that was it: wheat. It was a grain for grinding, or so the Wisdom said. He was curious to see how these plants grew and could not wait to sow them. He wondered if they would grow as quickly as the fruit trees. There was only one way to find out, and he set off in search of a suitable planting place.

Eira woke to find herself alone in the cave. Her parents had crept out not wishing to wake her. After all, they thought, she must be tired after such an adventure. In fact, Eira awoke feeling refreshed and eager to meet whatever the new day might bring. She walked to the door and breathed in the morning air. It had a strange fragrance and a clear coolness, which filled her head with its cold sharpness, making her feel intoxicated. *Drunk with the goodness of life*, she thought to herself, laughing quietly.

She dressed quickly and set out in search of her father. She suspected that he might have gone to find a suitable planting site for the rest of the seeds he had found in the crater, and she did not want to miss the excitement of seeing them placed gently in the earth. Her mother, she knew, would have gone with the other villagers to search for food, as they did every morning. But the sight that greeted her eyes as she ran up the cliff path made her stare in amazement. The sun, which was already riding high in a brilliantly blue sky, was shining warm and bright, and the ground beneath her feet was soft and springy with the touch of the short, coarse grass that had begun to grow on the cliff tops.

Great white gulls called to each other as they soared overhead. But there was something else too. Listening intently, her ears detected a subtler sound: the sound of buzzing insects! She could scarcely believe her senses. Perhaps she was still dreaming, she thought, as a butterfly as red as fire alighted on her arm, its exquisitely beautiful wings gently brushing her skin. No—no, this was real!

Exhilarated, she raced along the familiar paths searching for her father, but there was no sign of him anywhere. After a while she began to tire, so she flung herself down despondently on the warm ground to rest. Lulled by the gentle drone of many insects, she soon began to doze.

As she lay, drifting gently in and out of sleep, she became aware of something moving on her chest. Sleepily, her hand touched the amulet around her neck.Its snake-like body pulsed gently as if she were feeling its heartbeat. With a cry of alarm, she started awake.Looking down, she realised that she was holding the golden amulet. It was alive! The green eyes shone with a piercing brightness, and she could swear that the creature was breathing. With a gasp she let it drop from her hand and watched with amazement as the glittering object began to rotate, moving slowly at first, but with gradually increasing speed; until, try as she might, she could not keep it in sight as its motion had become a mere blur.

Hypnotised, she lost all awareness of her surroundings, until she heard a voice calling her. 'Eira, Eira, are you there? Can you see me? It's Aarush. Can you hear me?' The voice called again and again, until, as if fighting against some great force which held her eyelids tightly shut, she managed to prise them open. She found herself in a darkness so impenetrable that she could not even see her own hand stretched out in front of her. She appeared to be suspended in nothingness, and there was no sign of the amulet. But somewhere in the distance she could hear Aarush calling her.

She must try and find him. He was nearby; she was sure of it. Rising uncertainly to her feet, she found that she could move effortlessly in the inky darkness. All she had to do was to think of herself moving, and she could drift through the air with ease. 'Aarush,' she called, 'Aarush, it's me. I'm here. Where are you?'

Then in the distance, she saw something moving. It glinted softly. Willing herself towards the mysterious object, she peered through the blackness. As she drew closer, the outline of a great creature loomed into view, its golden body silhouetted against the impenetrable void which stretched out on all sides.

She willed herself closer to the great beast. Its golden scales glinted dully. Its eyes were aflame with a piercing green light so bright that it almost blinded her. She was drawn towards it with an almost unbearable longing. Something inside her seemed to urge her on. If she failed, she felt sure she would never see Aarush again. As she drew closer, she became aware of a low rumbling sound, which made her whole body shake and tremble. A gentle breeze created by the creature's motion ruffled her hair. The amulet around her neck seemed to be moving too, pulsing with a heart-like beat. The metal against her chest was warm, and the closer she got to the rotating giant the hotter it became, until it almost burned her skin. The breeze became a gale. It keened and roared through the air as the monstrous serpent spun ever faster, until there was only a patch of white-hot light careering through space. The roaring became a whining, high-pitched whistling, which almost deafened her. She put her hands to her ears in a vain attempt to shut out the sound. As she did so, she found herself being drawn into the central space that the creature's body encircled and watching helplessly as the dazzling light rushed and flashed around her.

Fear gripped her, as she could no longer move at will. Desperately, she called out to Aarush to help her, and as she did so she saw him approaching what had become a great vortex of light. He had been there all along, on the other side of the creature. At that moment, he caught sight of her and held out his arms, but he too seemed unable to move any closer. They were suspended, helpless, trapped by the spinning body of the great serpent. Despair threatened to overwhelm her, and, just as she was about to give up and surrender herself to her fate, the deafening noise, the roaring, buffeting wind, and the almost unbearable heat disappeared, and she was floating peacefully in velvety stillness. The great beast too was still, its body glistening, somehow reflecting the hidden light of the shining blackness which surrounded them. Aarush was there too, and he was also floating gently, suspended close to the great creature, which seemed to be resting, breathing gently.

She no longer felt afraid, and as she floated a feeling of deep contentment filled her whole being. Somehow she knew that if she just let go and felt her longing for Aarush in her heart, she would reach him without effort. Now she understood! She could do nothing. She must allow herself to be taken, as in fact she had been all along, and Aarush must do the same. A comforting warmth enveloped her, and she closed her eyes, letting herself drift on what felt like a warm ocean, which held her tenderly supported, its gentle current drawing her along.

'Eira,' the voice said gently, 'Eira, open your eyes. It is I, the one you named Aarush. I am here. The time for sleeping is passed. Wake up. We are together at last!'

Eira opened her eyes to the sight of Aarush's face close to hers, his eyes shining with joy. *I must be dreaming*, she thought, and then she felt the warm grip of his hand in hers. *At last, we are together, and this time it is not a dream!* They were still floating, surrounded by the body of the great serpent, now still and quiet, its gaze fixed upon the pair, as if it were watching over them, waiting.

* * *

Invigorated by the unaccustomed warmth and the freshness of the air blowing off a now calm and tranquil sea, Adil set off at a brisk pace up the cliff path. He intended to head inland a little way to where the ground was flatter and more sheltered from the sea breezes. Finally, after much searching, he found a place which met his needs. It was a large area of even ground, now covered in coarse, wiry grass. It was a good thing he had brought a digging implement with him, he thought to himself, as he would have to clear the ground first before he could plant the seeds.

Digging was hot, slow work, and it took him some time to clear an area large enough to give the seeds room to sprout and grow without being crowded by the now vigorous grass. At last, it was finished and he reached into his pocket and took out the tiny handful of blackened seeds. He was just about to begin placing them in the ground, when he remembered that Eira had wanted to be with him when he planted the wheat seeds. He looked around for signs of his daughter, but she was nowhere to be seen. He called out to her, but there was no reply. Everything was quiet, strangely quiet, he thought to himself. He could no longer hear the plaintive cry of gulls on the cliff or the sleepy buzzing of insects, nor even the sound of the sea gently sighing, as it trickled its way up the shingle beach then retreated, folding in upon itself once more.

Clouds drifted slowly across the face of the sun, filling the sky with a misty haze. He must find Bethan and Eira, he thought urgently. Something was wrong; they might be in danger. But first he must finish what he came here to do. Somehow, at that moment, it seemed to be the most important thing in the world. He must plant the seeds! Stooping, he made several small holes, and quickly dropped a single seed into each one. Gently, he covered them over with a layer of soil. It was done, he thought with satisfaction. Now he must find his wife and daughter!

Almost running back down the gentle slope that led to the cliff path, he called out, 'Bethan, Eira, can you hear me? Where are you?' But there was no reply.

When he reached the place where Bethan and the other villagers usually started their day's foraging, it was deserted. He ran about, frantically searching behind every rock, but there was no one there. Perhaps they had gone home, he thought. Yes, that must be it, they had found all the food they needed, and they had all gone home early. But as he turned, intending to take the homeward path, he saw a sight which rooted him to the spot.

Rolling across the sea towards him, drifting in great white banks, was an enormous sheet of cloud. It was not the thin, evil-smelling grey mist that drifted near the ground, clinging to everything it touched. No, this was a thick, impenetrable sheet of pure white which looked for all the world as if it were solid and not a mist at all. As he watched, he began to feel its icy cold tendrils on his skin. He shivered, but somehow he seemed unable to move, as the fog enveloped him like a great, white blanket. He gasped as he breathed in its icy coldness. Frantically, he struggled against the cold and an increasingly strong desire to close his eyes and sleep. And then, just as panic began to overtake him, he felt rather than heard a gentle voice saying, 'Do not be afraid; you have nothing to fear. Rest in the arms of my all concealing blanket. When you awake, all will be well. That is my promise.'

Soothed by the voice, Adil closed his eyes, and as he did so he felt the coldness disappear and in its place a comforting warmth surrounded him. He seemed to be floating, cushioned by something so soft and light as to be almost imperceptible. He longed to open his eyes and look at his surroundings, but try as he might he could not part his eyelids, and they remained firmly shut.

* * *

Bethan had joined the other villagers for their daily foraging trip. They were all in good spirits, laughing and joking as they searched the rapidly growing grassland for food. As the grass grew thicker, the ground nuts became more difficult to find, but other, more palatable foods had begun to appear, and they spent the whole morning marvelling at the new and plentiful morsels they found, eagerly tasting each new discovery.

The air was getting cold again, Bethan thought, shivering and rubbing her arms. Looking with satisfaction at her basket, which was now full to the brim with all kinds of roots and herbs, she decided to finish for the day and make her way home. Calling her farewells to her companions, some of whom were sitting enjoying the midday sunshine, she began the steep descent back to the village.

She smiled appreciatively as she watched the sunlight reflecting off the sea, dancing and sparkling like a thousand tiny stars. But the horizon had disappeared, obscured by an enormous bank of cloud, which was rolling towards the cliffs at incredible speed. It was pure white and reflected the fading sunlight, so that its brightness dazzled her. Puzzled, she stood watching it for several minutes. What could possibly be causing such a thing? The air was growing increasingly cold. She would go and light a fire. Adil and

Eira would doubtless be home soon too. But the path seemed steeper than usual, and the cold air caught in her throat, making her cough. She gasped for breath and everything around her started to spin. Gritting her teeth, she somehow managed to keep her balance and staggered the last few yards to the cave entrance, where she flung herself down onto the floor, breathing heavily. Time enough to light the fire when she had recovered herself, she thought, as her eyes closed and a soothing warmth engulfed her. Then she was drifting, drifting on a sea of softness.

Outside the cave, the thick blanket of dense, white cloud had engulfed the land, and every living thing lay sleeping peacefully where it had fallen. Even the great white gulls that moments before had been soaring on the cliff top, were sitting, their sharp yellow beaks tucked beneath their folded wings, eyes closed, fast asleep.

It was cold, very cold, but the sleepers did not seem to feel it, as they lay breathing gently. An eerie silence filled the air. Not a sound could be heard, not a creature called or cried out. Even the sea was silent, the sound of the waves breaking on the shore somehow subdued, inaudible. Not a breath of wind stirred the air.

* * *

Tenebrae stood watching the approaching cloud. It was still daylight, but somehow this did not seem to matter anymore. He felt its warmth and the dying rays of the sun, but they no longer burned his eyes and skin. He could see the land around him as clearly as if it were the darkest night. The rest of his people were more cautious and had not dared to venture out into the light to watch the great cloud approaching. But Tenebrae remembered the Prophecy, and he hoped with all his heart that this was the sign that he had longed to see but had never dared to imagine would come in his lifetime.

Many years ago, when he was but a young cub, he had travelled to the seashore and ventured deep into the caves that ran under the cliffs. There he had seen the paintings that his people had made long ago: the images of the man and the woman and the curling serpent with the green eyes. The woman, whose likeness he had seen in the face of the girl in the stone circle, was the Chosen One, he felt sure. She had not been afraid of him and had shown him compassion. And now, if the Prophecy was to be fulfilled at last, his people would walk unafraid in the light of day and stand with pride alongside the race of men.

The great cloud drew nearer, and he felt its coldness as it approached. Accustomed though he was to the cold, dark places of the earth, its chill made him shiver. Perhaps he should return to his people, as they might be afraid. Making his way back down the tunnel to where the rest of the Noctu waited, he felt chill fingers grip his shoulders, and a sudden coldness filled his lungs. Coughing and choking, he ran down the passageway in an attempt to escape the pursuing mist. But it was too late, for there, lying on the ground, sleeping deeply, were his people. The stone floor beneath his feet seemed to sway, rising up to meet him, and the mist closed around the Chief of the Noctu, as it took him too in its slumberous embrace.

Chapter 13

A arush and Eira remained together, hand in hand, surrounded by the body of the great serpent. Neither of them were aware of the passing of time, somehow that did not seem to matter here. They were content to be together, suspended in the comforting stillness, surrounded by the deep darkness. They felt no fear, nor did they have any thoughts of the past nor indeed what was to become of them in the future. All was well, and nothing else mattered.

Presently, Eira felt Aarush's hand tighten around hers. He was staring straight ahead, peering intently into the bright darkness that surrounded them.

'It is changing: the darkness is receding,' he said in an urgent whisper. As they watched, the impenetrable blackness began to lighten, until it became the colour of darkest midnight blue. Faint pinpricks of light began to appear, growing brighter and brighter, until the lightening void was filled with a myriad stars, all casting their radiance upon the human pair. The great, golden serpent began to fade, and they felt firm ground beneath their feet once more. The stars no longer surrounded them but shone in a rapidly lightening sky. Then they too were gone, and the first rosy glow of a swift sunrise appeared on the horizon, illuminating the world around them. They found themselves standing in the stone circle where they had first met, but they were alone. There was no sign of the Guardians or their dwellings.

Looking around, they saw that the land was fresh and green. Trees burst into leaf as they watched. Great swathes of fragrant flowers covered the ground, filling the air with their perfume. The busy drone of bees and other insects could be heard everywhere. Beyond the great stones, a vast forest grew, and standing watching them from its margins was a huge stag, his great antlers casting strange shadows on the lightening ground.

Eira felt her whole being flood with awe and wonder, until she felt so light that she fancied she was floating gently, feet softly skimming the surface of the bright, green grass. Turning to Aarush, she said, 'This is your world, Aarush, isn't it? We have returned to your world.'

Aarush was silent for a moment as if listening, and then he said, 'No, this is not my world, at least not as it used to be. Your world and mine have merged and become one. The old and the new have united, just as you and I are together. My world has healed the wounds of your old, damaged world and brought new life with it; and your world has imparted wisdom to my young, fresh world; and so the two have gifted each other with life and wisdom. Something new has been born.'

'Something beautiful!' Eira whispered.

'Yes,' he answered smiling, 'and the amulets have returned to their resting place deep beneath the earth, ready for the day when they will be needed again.'

Eira felt around her neck and realised for the first time that the amulet had indeed disappeared, and looking at Aarush she saw that his too was gone. They had served their purpose in guiding her to Aarush and protecting them both, but she could not help feeling a little regret for their loss. She knew that he was right and that the symbols must return to their place beneath the earth, for perhaps, sometime in the far distant future, there would be another Eira and another Aarush, and they too would need the aid of the amulets.

The days that followed were filled with new discoveries for Eira. Aarush showed her where to find food, which fruits were the tastiest, where the purest water flowed, and, best of all, he introduced her to some of his animal companions, all of whom showed no fear of her. In fact some of the deer took to following her around, and when she stopped to rest they would come and push their soft muzzles into her hand, encouraging her to caress their heads as they watched her with their gentle, brown eyes.

She and Aarush spent many hours telling each other of how they used to spend their lives in the Alone Time, as they now called it. Aarush told her of the forest and how he had lived there alone for a time without reckoning. In fact, he could not remember a time when he had not lived there. Eira listened, fascinated, as he recounted his dreams of the strange, metal animals careering along straight, grey tracks and flying high in the air, creating terror amongst the other flying creatures; and of the sad people, who lived in the large, square caves, and how these dreams had puzzled and frightened him so much.

When Eira heard these stories, she recognised the world of the Before People, and she told Aarush how they had grown so arrogant that they had destroyed the beauty of the world and, in the end, themselves as well. It was into this poor, dead world that she had been born, she and a few others who struggled to live in its grey darkness. Then she told him of the Noctu and their Chieftain, Tenebrae. He listened intently when she told him this story: how the Noctu were a race of slaves that the Before People had created by corrupting the matrix of life itself; and how, when they finally destroyed themselves, these unfortunate creatures were left hiding deep within the dark places of the earth, objects of fear and hatred to the small, beleaguered band of humanity that remained, unable to bear the light of day even in that darkened world.

Wrinkling his brow, Aarush concentrated, straining to hear, then he said, 'The Wisdom speaks more softly as the days go by. The voice of the Great Guardian is fading,' he added sadly. 'We are to look for wisdom within ourselves for a while, although the Greatest Knower will never desert us. But these Noctu that you speak of are no longer to dwell in the dark places but will walk in the fullness of day along with humans, although they will be a race apart from us.'

Eira nodded solemnly, remembering the kindness the Noctu Chieftain had shown her and her father, when he had guided them through the ruins of the Great Barrier, and how he had shared his meagre food with them. Her father had told her of how a Noctus had spared his life that day in the tunnel, and dimly she remembered a shadowy figure bending over her as she lay unconscious in the stone circle the night before she and Aarush met there. She was glad that they would no longer be creatures of the shadow. She would teach her people not to fear them, and perhaps then the two races could live in peace together.

As she remembered that night at the stone circle, thoughts of her parents came flooding back. She had been so happy these last few days—exploring this beautiful new world, discovering its secrets, and, most of all, revelling in the company of her new-found companion, Aarush—that she had all but forgotten her family. Now she remembered them with a sudden rush of regret and alarm. Where were they? What had happened to them? Perhaps Aarush would ask the Wisdom for her, she thought.

Turning to him, she said tearfully, 'I long to see my parents again. I am afraid of what might have happened to them when our two worlds merged.'

Seeing the sadness in her eyes, Aarush put his arms around her to console her, gently caressing her hair, and murmured, 'You are not alone, Eira. You have me and our forest companions.'

'But, Aarush,' she said, tears pricking her eyes, 'you don't understand what it is like to have a mother and a father and to know others of your kind. Please ask the Wisdom where my parents are.'

Aarush looked at his feet. 'Yes, you are right: I do not know these things. But as it causes you such pain to be without them, it is my dearest wish to restore them to you, if it is within my power.' He closed his eyes and was silent for what seemed to Eira like an eternity. Finally he raised his head, his eyes shining with happiness, and he laughed. 'It's all right! They are nearby! The Wisdom sent them into a deep sleep whilst the two worlds merged, but now they are awake. We are to go to the stone circle, where we shall find them waiting for us!'

Eira leapt to her feet and hugged Aarush so hard that he protested, saying that he could hardly breathe. 'Come on,' she said eagerly, grabbing him by the hand. 'We must hurry, or they will think that we're not coming! Oh, I can't wait to see Mother and Father again. I thought I'd lost them forever.'

Laughingly, Aarush got up from the rock on which he had been sitting and said, 'In that case, there is no time to lose. We must set out at once.'

By midday they had left the forest far behind, and a vast, open plain stretched out before them. There were no trees and the grass grew so tall that it almost reached their shoulders. They had to wade through it, pushing it aside as they went. Here and there the uniform green of the long grass was broken by small patches of red and yellow, where tall poppies peeped their heads above the lush grassland. Somewhere in the distance, they could hear the sound of a river as it flowed, chattering and crashing over rocks, but they could not see it, as it ran its course obscured by the giant grasses.

The pair paused, looking out across the great plain. Then Eira said suddenly, 'I know this place! This was where the last of the Before People died, and their bodies lay unburied for centuries until the earth covered them.It was called the Plain of the Dead. It is where Father and I fell into the crater, and where we found the seeds that he planted which grew into fruit trees overnight. Our path should take us past the trees, if they are still there. It seems almost a lifetime ago since we planted those few tiny, black seeds and watched them grow.'

'It *was* a lifetime ago,' said Aarush solemnly. 'You, me, and those who wait for us at the stone circle, all have a new life now; everything has been made whole again. Even this terrible place has been cleansed, and the echoes of the past have been erased. From now on, all can walk here without fear.'

Wading through the tall grass was exhausting work, and they were both hot, tired, and thirsty. Aarush stopped and listened for a moment. Then he said, 'I think we must be close to the river. Let's see if we can find it and quench our thirst.'

Eira bobbed her head above the grass and caught a glimpse of three young trees, growing not far from where they stood. 'I can see the trees, Aarush,' she said excitedly. 'They're growing over there,' and she pointed, mentally marking their location as she did so. They set off eagerly in search of the trees, both secretly hoping that they would find some fruit. But Aarush had been right about the river, and the next thing they knew they were both tumbling down a steep, grassy slope, finally coming to rest at the water's edge. Unhurt, they laughed, splashing each other with the cool water and taking great gulps of its refreshing sweetness.

When they had drunk their fill, they scrambled back up the river bank and made their way to the place where the three fruit trees grew, groaning with ripe fruit. The spring that Eira's father had used to water the seeds was still running down a crevice in the rock, which was now almost completely hidden by the tall grass. They sat and gorged themselves on the ripe fruit, savouring every sweet mouthful. When they had eaten, Eira began to clear the grass from around the base of the trees, and as she did so she made a solemn promise to come back every year and tend them.

'When we are old, our children will come here to watch over the trees, as they are a symbol of hope,' she said.

Aarush, who had never known want or hunger, looked with deep love and respect at her and whispered, 'It shall be so, for as long as the memory of these times remains within the hearts of those who come after us.'

Hand-in-hand, the pair continued their journey across the great plain, and as they walked Aarush said, 'This place shall no longer be called the Plain of the Dead, for those things have passed away. Death has been replaced with life. From now on, this place shall be called Espiron, for this is where the first seeds were planted and where the three trees of hope are growing.'

Eira smiled at him and said, 'This will always be

226

a special place. We shall bring our children here, and they will bring their children, and we shall tell them the tale of the three trees and how they grew and bore fruit in a single day. Do you think that they will believe us?' she added, laughing.

Of the wall, there was no trace. Not even a ridge remained on the ground to mark where it had once stood. The plain spread out before them, its surface completely flat, with not a sign that anything had ever been built there. *I wonder where the Noctu are now*, Eira mused. Aarush had said that they would live above the ground from now on. Maybe they too would be waiting for them at the stone circle.

Day was fading into night as they caught their first glimpse of the stone circle atop a slight rise in the ground, its huge, white stones outlined against the darkening sky. The smaller guiding stones, which used to mark the sacred way, had disappeared. All that remained was what had once been the inner circle of the stone sanctuary.

'It will be dark soon, and the Sanctuary is too far away for us to reach it today,' Aarush said. 'We must rest here for the night and complete our journey tomorrow. If we set out as the sun rises, we should be there by mid-morning.'

They made a small shelter out of sweet-smelling grasses and settled down for the night, lying on their backs, looking up at the star-filled sky and the landscape bathed in its clear light.

Chapter 14

Adil stretched and yawned widely. Slowly he opened his eyes, and for a moment he thought that he must still be asleep and dreaming, for the sight that met his eyes was familiar but at the same time totally new. He was lying in the centre of a great stone circle, much like the Sanctuary where he and Eira had visited his old friend Darius such a short time ago, or so it seemed. So much had happened since then that it felt as if a whole lifetime had passed since he sat in deep conversation with the Great Knower. Looking around, he could see a vast forest just beyond the outer boundary of the stone circle, and great swathes of tall grasses dotted with bright spots of colourful flowers carpeted the whole scene.

Rising to his feet a little shakily, as his limbs still felt unusually cold, he walked slowly over to one of the great stones, and there, to his utter astonishment, he made out the thin outline of what appeared to be writing. Excitedly, he scraped away the moss and lichen which covered most of the inscription, and, with difficulty as the writing was badly eroded in places as if it had been weathered by the passing of many years, he read the ancient text. As he did so, he realised that this inscription exactly matched the one carved on the great standing stones in the Sanctuary. How could this be? The writing here was indistinct and partially obscured by the passing of many centuries, but there was something familiar about the circle. Studying the other stones, he saw how one or two of them leaned over slightly, just as he remembered the ones in the inner circle of the Sanctuary had done. And there, up there on top of the other great stone which formed the processional entrance, there was that white patch of crystal in the shape of a bird! It was not possible, but it must be true. This was the Sanctuary, although the surrounding land was different, and there was no sign of the dwellings which had housed the Guardians. Only the circle itself remained, set in a landscape which was utterly changed, fresh and green, full of new life.

Bewildered, Adil made his way to the centre of the circle and almost fell over something lying on the ground. With a start, he saw that it was one of the villagers lying wrapped in deep sleep. Looking around, he realised that he was surrounded by the sleeping forms of many people. He must find Bethan and Eira, he thought urgently to himself. Surely they must be here too. Frantically, he ran from sleeper to sleeper, peering into their peaceful faces, hoping to see the familiar features of the two people he loved most in the world.

After much searching, he came upon the sleeping form of his wife. Gently he tried to rouse her. Eventually, after what seemed like an eternity to the anxious Adil, she opened her eyes and looked at him. At first he thought that she did not recognise him, but gradually she became more aware of her surroundings, and, rubbing her cold limbs with a shiver, she smiled at him and said, 'Where are we, Adil? This is not our home. How did we get here? What is this place? The last thing I remember, was seeing a great, white cloud coming towards me, and feeling myself overwhelmed by an icy coldness. Then I was slipping into sleep, and someone was holding my hand, leading me to a place which was soft and warm and safe, and where a voice whispered gently that I should just rest here for a while, that everything was going to be all right.'

'Mmm,' Adil murmured, 'I had a similar experience myself. But to answer your question, I think we are at the Sanctuary, although it is much changed since I saw it last, and there is no sign of Darius or the Guardians. But perhaps they are amongst the sleepers.'

'Yes, husband, I have heard you talk many times of this place, and it is beautiful,' Bethan said, looking around her at the majestic stones that surrounded them, and drinking in the sight of the soft, green grass and the distant forest. Gratefully, she took a deep breath, inhaling the fragrant air.

A soft breeze had sprung up, and it blew away the last thin wisps of white mist, revealing a bright blue sky. The sun was warm on their faces as they sat quietly, hand-in-hand, each grateful for the presence of the other. Slowly, revived by the warm sunshine and refreshed by the gentle breeze, the other sleepers were awakening, rising uncertainly to their feet and gazing sleepily around them. Bethan and Adil recognised the familiar faces of their friends and neighbours from the village and some of the younger Guardians, but neither Eira nor Darius were among them.

One by one, the villagers caught sight of the pair, and soon they were surrounded by a small crowd all talking at once.

'Adil, respected Knower, where are we? How did we come to be here? What is this place?'

Adil rose to his feet and signed for them to be quiet. 'Please, please, my friends! All in good time. All in good time. We are, I think, in the Sanctuary, or at least what was once the Sanctuary, although the Great Knower, Darius, is not with us. As to why we are here, or how we got here, I am no wiser than you. But I feel sure that the Great Power that brought us will, in time, make everything clear. In the meantime, I suggest you rest and enjoy the good things that our new surroundings have to offer.'

Satisfied, at least for the moment, the crowd began to disperse and wander off in search of food, the younger members of the group running excitedly ahead, eager to explore this fresh new world. Adil breathed a sigh of relief and turned to Bethan. 'We must find Eira,' he said anxiously. She was not with the other villagers, so where could she be? As he turned towards the path, he glimpsed a dark shape flit between two of the tall outer stones. Shading his eyes against the sun, he peered into the shadows, but he could see nothing. *It must have been my imagination*, he thought, and with a dismissive shrug, he led Bethan along the old, familiar processional path in search of their daughter.

For several hours they wandered around the sacred hill, searching, calling, hoping that Eira would hear them. Perhaps she had fallen asleep some distance from here and did not know that they were all gathered at the Sanctuary. But they, too, had been overtaken by the mist far from this place. Adil turned to Bethan, distraught as the terrible thought dawned on him. Perhaps Eira was not to share in this new world. She, who had dreamt of the Prophecy and a fresh new world. No, it could not be! She must be part of it. He could not believe that the Great Guardian would cause it to be otherwise. But where was she?

Just as he felt that he couldn't bear the terrible un-certainty any longer, he felt a gentle touch on his arm. It was Bethan.

'My dear,' she said quietly, 'don't fret; our daughter is safe, of that I am certain. She will be with us soon. We must be patient. For when she comes, all will be complete, and we can truly begin our new lives together.'

Adil sighed, thinking that Bethan sought only to reassure him, but then he saw how her eyes shone with joy and certainty. She knew that what she said was true.

'You are right, my dear, we must be patient. She will come when she can,' he said, taking his wife's hand almost reverently. 'In the meantime, let us go and look for the old settlement. Perhaps Darius is waiting there.'

The two set off hand-in-hand, searching for signs of

the old Guardian settlement, but nothing remained. Not a single stone, stick of furniture, or cooking pot did they find. All had vanished without a trace, along with Darius and some of the older Guardians. Adil was saddened that his old friend was not there to see and enjoy the beautiful new world that they had woken into. The old Knower would have been overjoyed to see the Prophecy fulfilled. But then he remembered his parting words, when he and Eira had taken their leave, before setting off on what had proved to be such a perilous journey home. He sighed as he pictured the face of his wise old friend. The memory was so fresh, it seemed like only yesterday. 'I grow old, Adil dear friend, and will not live to see the Prophecy fulfilled. My time has passed. Now is the time of the new and the young. Be glad for them and for those you leave behind, as their work is done and they can go peacefully to their rest.'

Smiling ruefully to himself, Adil fought back the tears. Darius had known all along that he and some of the older Guardians would not enter the new world but that his life had not been in vain. All he had spent a lifetime protecting had come to fruition, and that was enough for him. He accepted that he would not see his life's work completed. He trusted, knew with an unshakeable certainty, that the Prophecy was about to be fulfilled. He had read the signs and was content.

Suddenly, Adil was shaken from his reverie by a rattling, rustling sound coming from a small group of bushes nearby. Scanning the shrubbery, he could see nothing. But there it was again! A dark shadow fell across the ground in front of him. It had the outline of a tall man. Spinning around in alarm, he found himself looking straight into the eyes of Tenebrae, Chief of the Noctu.

'Greetings, Adil, respected Knower. We meet again but this time in the bright light of day. The sun's rays reveal all; nothing can escape its penetrating gaze. I stand before you a free being. Free to walk in daylight and to lead my people as a race equal to mankind.'

Adil stood, staring at the Noctu leader, speechless. Gone was the shambling, cringing creature that shunned the slightest glimmer of daylight, an air of foulness and decay surrounding him. Here he stood, erect, tall, and imposing, his strong features tranquil and at peace, pride and dignity shining from his eyes, which gazed at the daylight world fearlessly, no longer dazzled by the light. *So*, he thought, *there are to be two sentient races in this fresh new world*, and he felt a sense of joy rising in his heart. The Noctu had truly earned their place as equals beside men, their former tormentors, after centuries of suffering and persecution, and he was glad. But he was not so sure that mankind was worthy of their place in this new world. After all, they had been responsible for its destruction once before. Had they truly learned from their mistakes? Could they fulfil their trust this time? Perhaps the Noctu would hold them to their responsibilities? This once despised but now noble race would act as a constant reminder of the evil that first brought them into being, and as a symbol of hope. Even the vilest of things can be transformed and made whole in the end. From the moment of its inception, everything contains the seed of renewal within it. There is always hope.

Adil bowed his head to the Noctu Chief in reverent greeting. 'Tenebrae, welcome to this sacred place. The world has changed, and you with it.'

Tenebrae laughed, a deep sonorous, horn-like laugh, filled with the deep places of the earth, dark and earthy, but at the same time full of the richness of growing things. 'Honoured Knower, it is not only I who have changed. You too are different! It is as if a hundred winters have been wiped from your face and body! Together we shall walk the wild places of this new world, as friends and equals. We have much to learn from each other. But that is for the future. For now, we await the coming of the One and her Mate, for all is not complete until they are with us'.

Puzzled, Adil asked, 'Of whom do you speak?'

Tenebrae laughed his deep-throated laugh. 'You know only too well who she is, for you gave her life.'

'Eira? Do you speak of my daughter, Eira?' Adil gasped. Of course, he should have realised; he knew the Prophecy. He had seen the signs, listened to his daughter's dreams, and been with her that day at the Sanctuary. But how did Tenebrae know these things? He who had spent his life in the dank, dark places of the earth. Looking at the dignified, ennobled creature that stood before him, he realised with a jolt of shame that he and his race were not a privileged kind. All races and all creatures served the Great Guardian, whose Wisdom encompassed all things. Humbled by this realisation, he could only nod dumbly and watch as the Noctu leader bowed courteously and strode across the stone circle to join the rest of his people where they waited, tall, erect, and eager for the coming of the Chosen One, his daughter, Eira.

* * *

As Eira opened her eyes, the first pale streaks of daylight were stealing across the sky, which glowed a warm pink as the sun began its daily ascent, rising slowly above the horizon, gradually illuminating more and more of the landscape as it did so. She gasped in awe at the sight. *How beautiful it all is*, she thought. As she sat watching the dawn of a new day, she felt Aarush stir beside her. The sight of the rising sun was not new to him. He had seen a thousand sunrises, each as beautiful as the last, but to Eira it was still a new and very moving experience. She treasured every moment and did not want to miss a single detail.

Tearing herself reluctantly away from the beauty of the sunrise, Eira turned to Aarush. 'We should not delay our journey any longer,' she said, feeling a sudden sense of urgency. She was eager to see her parents again, and Aarush had said the Wisdom had told him that a great company awaited them. She hoped desperately that her mother and father were amongst them. Nodding in agreement, he rose quickly to his feet and soon they were wading through the long grass, heading directly for the stone circle, which was dimly visible in the hazy morning sunshine atop the far hill.

The sun was already riding high in the sky by the time they reached the old processional way. Another hour and they would reach the stone circle. 'We should be there by midday,' Aarush said. A thick, springy turf, which felt soft beneath their feet, now covered the once cinder-grey rubble of the hill. As they reached the top, Eira caught sight of a great forest growing on the far side. There had been no forest there when she and her father had visited Darius just a few short months ago, she thought. Although, for her, so little time seemed to have passed since her last visit to this place, everything had changed so much that one could imagine the passing of centuries.

At last they reached the outer markers. The sound of voices talking quietly, respectfully, drifted on the air, although they could not see the speakers as the hill rose sharply at this point, just before the path passed between the first stones, causing them to be hidden from view. As they drew closer, they could make out many different voices, some strangely deep and unfamiliar. It sounded as if a great company had gathered. Eira shivered with anticipation and grasped Aarush's hand nervously.

As the pair crested the hill, a voice called out excitedly, 'I see them. They're here!' A loud clamour of greeting arose, echoing around that ancient place in such a way that it seemed as if there were many thousands present, instead of the small crowd that surged forward eagerly to greet them as they approached.

Leading the group were Bethan and Adil, who stared at their daughter in amazement. Could this dignified young woman, her face shining with newly found wisdom, really be their daughter? She walked beside the man they knew to be Aarush, and the couple held themselves with a dignity and authority which caused Eira's parents to hesitate before greeting them. Adil could only gape in amazement, as he saw standing before him the royal pair from the painting in the cave, and yet here they were, living and breathing! Bethan's delight at seeing her daughter alive and well and finally united with the mysterious stranger from her dreams was too much for her, and she flung her arms joyfully around her, exclaiming that she had thought they would never see her again. Then remembering themselves, both she and Adil bowed respectfully to Aarush, who greeted them a little shyly. He was, after all, not used to company! As the little family stood united once more, tears of joy running down their cheeks and surrounded by many smiling faces, there was a stir in the crowd, which parted to allow a tall, upright figure to approach the pair.

Tenebrae stood before them, erect, dignified, his eyes shining with admiration and respect. 'So, at last the Prophecy has been fulfilled, and the Chosen One has found her Mate. All has been healed and restored,' he said, his sonorous voice so deep that it caused the very stones to shake. 'We, the race of Noctu, are grateful to you for the part you have played in our rising, and we shall not forget it. Our young cubs will hear of how the One, guided by the tail of the serpent, followed her dreams and found the Stranger who Waits, and how they were united and a new, fresh world came into being. They shall learn of how our people were raised, their dignity restored, old wounds healed and old wrongs forgotten, buried forever in the past. May our two peoples live together in harmony for as long as this memory remains in our hearts. We go now to begin our new life, walking fearlessly in the clear light of day.'

'Chief Tenebrae, will you and your people not stay and join us as we celebrate the dawning of a new age?' Eira said, raising her voice to be heard above the clamour of the crowd.

'Let the Chosen One speak!' someone shouted. The crowd fell silent.

'You would honour us by your presence,' Eira continued.

Chief Tenebrae bowed low. 'It is you who honour us! Please forgive our rough ways. We are accustomed to avoiding the company of our fellow creatures, and old habits die hard. It would be our pleasure to join this noble gathering,' he said turning to his people, who solemnly nodded in agreement. The Noctu leader had hardly finished speaking when a great cheer and shouts of welcome went up from the crowd. Bowing low to Eira and Aarush, he led his people to the stone circle, where they seated themselves and began to sing. Their voices, deep and strangely melodious, filled the air, causing the great stones to vibrate until they too seemed to sing.

The villagers stood open-mouthed, staring at the fledgling race in wonder. But soon, drawn by the magic of the Noctu voices, they joined their new cousins amongst the stones, and they too began to sing some of their own songs. Eira turned to Aarush, her face shining with happiness. 'We do not have songs for such an occasion as this. This is a time for new songs and new stories. The old ways are finished, and a new life has been born. The serpent has completed the circle, and all has been renewed once more. For this is not an ending but a new beginning.'

Silently she took Aarush's hand in hers and together they walked into the centre of the circle, where they were soon surrounded by villagers and Noctu alike, as they added their own voices to the sounds of rejoicing.

About the Author

TANIA HENZELL-THOMAS has always been an avid reader of fantasy and mythic literature, enjoying stories that uplift and inspire the reader. She especially values the genre of imaginative fantasy because it is a vividly concrete and accessible way of conveying deep spiritual truths. Writing on an archetypal level frees the reader from the everyday world and transports them to an expansive place beyond the mundane, where they can meet, personified, some of the underlying principles which guide and enrich our deepest selves.

She is inspired by her love of the natural world and, at a time when many are becoming increasingly disconnected from their environment, she seeks to evoke in her writing a sense of our profoundly deep bond with nature and, increasingly, with the worlds that lie waiting to be discovered beyond our own small planet.